A NOTE FROM THE AUTHOR

Finding You Finding Me is a mash up of contemporary fiction and romantic fantasy (not fantasy as in fantasy romance and the other kinds of fantasy books I write, but fantasy in that some situations...um...some of the poses are not encouraged in public or would garner you a ticket for public indecency).

Due to some of the mature themes contained in this novel, this novel is suggested for young adults, new adults, age 18 and older. If you are easily offended by some language, steamy scenes, and adult social situations, then this book is not for you.

I sincerely hope you will enjoy Sam's story. I am honored that you chose to read it. Happy Daggers Dreams...

Sincerely,

Kailin

Finding You

Finding Me

A You & Me Trilogy Book

kailin gow

Kailin Gow

Finding You Finding Me
Published by
Sparklesoup Inc.
Copyright © 2013 Kailin Gow

For information, please contact:
www.sparklesoup.com
First Edition.
ISBN: 978-1597480543

DEDICATION

To All the Women Who Took Back the Night.

And the men who love them.

To all the women who supported this book series and told me to trust my artistic voice so Sam's story of being found could be told uncensored and uncut, right from the start.

Acknowledgements

To the ladies of Naughty Mafia – Michelle Valentine, Emily Snow, Katie Ashley, Kristen Proby, and Kelli Maine; thank you for including me in all the mayhem and fun. We are going to rock Vegas this year.

Kailin Gow

To Kendall Ryan, fun times ahead...looking forward to it!

To Sylvia Day and EL James, thank you for paving the way for indies, especially other indie authors of romance fiction. Your kindness in sharing your advice and expertise to us newbies in adult romance fiction is greatly appreciated.

To all the bloggers and readers who have been so supportive of me and my books, getting the word out and suggesting my books to friends and family; thank you from the bottom of my heart. I love each and every one of you!

To my editors at Sparklesoup.com, thank you for your patience. I'm working on the next book as fast as I can!

Prologue

There comes a time in life when you have to make that decision that you know will determine the course of the rest of your life. Those are the hard decisions buried between the lines of black and white and hidden so deep within the murky blur of charcoal grey that it takes heavy scrubbing to uncover the gem within.

Today was that time for me...the day I go searching for that hidden gem of truth. The time when I know there was this decision I have to make, that could not be reversible, a decision that would change who I was and where I was heading. Black and white. White and black. Crossing the lines would make things grey. Was I prepared to turn this shade, was I prepared for this change?

My hands shook as I handed the envelope to the lady at the post office. "How long will it take to get there?" I asked.

"A few days," the friendly-faced Asian woman behind the post office counter said. "It's being sent Priority so it will get there faster. Did you need to send it faster?"

"No, no," I said. "That's soon enough."

I hesitated.

The woman finished stamping the envelope and was about to throw it into the bin behind her when I shot out my hand to stop her.

"Wait," I said. "I changed my mind."

Startled, the woman asked. "Are you sure?"

"Yes," I nodded. "I'm sure."

She handed the thick envelope back to me, which I deposited into my shoulder bag. I handed her some cash and quickly shot out of there, feeling the need for some fresh air.

It was a simple enough act for me to retrieve my envelope, but acknowledging to myself that I didn't go through with it was something else entirely.

Finding You Finding Me (You & Me Trilogy #2)

It meant that instead of choosing the path I was supposed to take, I chose the latter. The one that I was not supposed to take, the one that every ounce of my five foot five frame was scared to death to take…

I was supposed to mail out that envelope. I was supposed to move on with my life and follow the rules, like the Valedictorian straight A Pastor's kid that I was. The girl who seemed to have it all – a beautiful family, a scholarship to Stanford, and now a closet full of tapes.

Collins McGregor's tapes.

Beautifully flawed, handsome, and sexy hot beyond belief Collins McGregor's hidden tapes, meant only for his eyes. And now mine. The tapes from which I could not tear my eyes away. The tapes I found myself wanting to be part of, had even began dreaming about, with me in it, as well as Collins McGregor.

I shook my head. The mere thought of him had me blushing. Thank God I was already in my car, flushed with the thoughts of Collins and those tapes. Collins McGregor had only been away in Europe for a couple of months, opening up a new subsidiary for his billion dollar entertainment and media enterprise, The Collins Companies, but it felt like forever. The effects of his last kiss on my lips from months ago still linger, and I knew deep within me that was one reason why I didn't send that envelope.

My rational side knew I should mail off my response, move on and out so I can accomplish what my mind had set out to do to achieve the kind of life I had dreamed of, but my impulsive emotion-laden side didn't care, reacting quickly to snatch the envelope back, not caring about the consequences, but only of my needs. Which at this moment, consisted mostly of food, water, and Collins.

Oh Collins. I'm as deeply buried in this as you are.

The thought terrified me. I should be running away from all of it, as Collins himself told me to do, but since he gave me that key to his safe deposit box and gave me the choice to back off or to move forward, I couldn't help wanting and needing more. I've had a taste of Collins McGregor. He's let me in. He's given me his key not only to his safe deposit box, but to his deep dark secretive world. The world he's tried to leave behind for me, but couldn't. I should back away and run, but I couldn't. I should cut myself off completely from Collins, but I can't.

Something inside of me called out and craved this part of Collins, something that so desperately needed this sordidness, as though it was an answer to a deep dark mystery within that I needed to find. Whatever it was, I couldn't turn back. With Collins McGregor, it was either black or white, never anything in between. No shades of grey here, just a journey from white to black, or was it the other way around?

*****

I was halfway to Sawyer House, the teen and young adult crisis center I volunteered at as a peer counselor when I heard the familiar ringtone on my phone going off.

Kailin Gow

Pachelbel's Canon in D Major.

It was familiar, but also a surprise…haven't been used in weeks.

I was exhilarated hearing it go off, but nervous at the same time.

I let it ring for a little while before summoning my strength to answer. "Hi," I said, my voice instinctively turning breathy and an octave lower.

"Hi," he said in an equally breathy tone. It was as deep, yet soft and velvety as I remembered. Downright sexy as hell. "Today's the day," he said. "Have you decided, Sam?"

"Yes," I said softly. "I have."

"I've been waiting for months for this," he said. "I can't wait any longer."

"You don't have to," I said. "I watched your tapes. I watched all of it. Everything."

There was a soft gasp at the other end of the phone, one that made my stomach flutter. Daggers. Soft and vulnerable Daggers. Even in Europe, so far away from where I was in Newport Beach, California, I can feel his boyish vulnerability, feel his pain and insecurity. By giving me those tapes, by trusting me with them, he had opened himself widely to me. He had opened up and cut through all the deep layers within him, the many layers that made up the beautiful and powerful, but deeply pained man that he was. It was not an easy thing for him to do, and no matter what my answer would be, I would always appreciate Collins for trusting me with his secret.

He didn't say anything for a while.

I didn't say anything for a while. It would take a lot for me to make the next move and answer him, but it was something I had to do for him, and for me.

"I," I started. "I'm not going."

"You're not going?" he asked.

"No, Collins, I'm not."

"It's what you dreamed of," he said.

"Still dreamed of," I said, "but some things are better left there."

"You should go, you know," he said.

"I've decided not to," I said.

"Why?" he asked. "I thought you've always wanted to go to Stanford."

"Things change," I said quickly.

"So you don't need the scholarship," he said.

"No," I answered. "I'm not taking it. Nor am I taking your money."

"Sam," Collins tone changed immediately. Harsher, more insistent. "You'll need it for whatever you decide to go into. It's yours to keep."

I swallowed. Collins was being so generous right now and I never would take advantage of that generosity. "No, I'm not taking it, Collins."

"If you're not taking it, then I assume you're agreeing to the other condition of my proposition," he said in all seriousness but with a hint of wicked amusement in his voice.

"I've seen your tapes, Collins," I said, barely a whisper, "and I can't seem to stop thinking about it and about you."

Another gasp, but this time, deeper and more in charge. "Sam, you do know what you're getting into, don't you?"

"Yes," I said, feeling an inferno of heat shoot through me as I answered him.

"And you still want to be with me...after this discovery?"

"Yes," I said again, feeling bolder from hearing his voice, as if hypnotized.

"Then, Samantha Sullivan, my dear sweet girl," Collins said. "I can't wait to see you in an hour."

Chapter 1

"An hour?" I protested. "But you're in Europe."

"Apparently I'm not," Collins said. "I didn't forget today was the day. Believe it or not, Sam, I would make a special return flight home just to hear your decision whispered into my ears in person. Clear your schedule, Sam. I'll be at your house in about an hour."

"But I have to be at Sawyer House," I said. "I'm training a new counselor today."

"Have you taken the place of that man boy as trainer?" Collins asked, slightly amused. "I wouldn't be surprised if you do, Sam."

"Derek," I said. "No, I won't be replacing him," I smiled into the phone, thinking about the handsome trainer at Sawyer House who quickly became my friend months ago and had become my closest friend in the last couple of months since Collins left. A psychology major at the University of California at Irvine, he had taken me under his wings, at Sawyer House, training me and giving me advice on some of the social situations that came up there during the intense calls. Just a couple of years older than I, but more experienced and worldly than I was because of his college experience and upbringing, being raised by a single mother in a rougher part of town, he also tried to show me a little more of the world. Given how sheltered I was because of my upbringing, it opened my eyes a bit. But when it came to knowing everything about the world and its hidden riches and secrets, no one was like Collins McGregor…my beautiful, but raw and edgy billionaire boy wonder/former lover.

"Then he's still there," Collins said, his voice dripping with annoyance.

"Well…you and I," I said. "You broke up with me and…"

"Are you two together?" Collins' voice was as cold as ice. A complete switch from warmly seductive to murderous steel. "You got together with him as soon as the opportunity…"

"No, not together," I said, feeling defensive. It was no secret to Collins and I that Derek wanted a lot more than friendship with me, and had tried in the past to get there.

"I wouldn't put it past him to try," Collins said. "But I know you, Sam. If you were to ever find yourself in a position to be thoroughly fucked, it wouldn't be with him."

Anger flashed through me then. How dare he use that against me. How dare he throw my deep-seated terror of intimacy into my face. "Oh, you think you know that about me?" I said icily.

"I know it takes someone stronger than Mr. Psych to break through your wall, Sam," Collins said. "Someone who knows how to heat up that inner passion of yours to the point you just don't care how you get fucked or when, but that you do, and that's all that you can think of."

I felt the heat rising in me as the intensity of his words burn through the waves through my ear and into my core, running down to my lower body where I felt myself shiver with desire.

Finding You Finding Me (You & Me Trilogy #2)

"You're feeling it right now, aren't you, Sam?" Collins said. "The need? Your need to be thoroughly and deeply fucked by me. I can think of many imaginative ways to do it, too. You're feeling the tingling in you that starts below. Is it hot or is it cold? Is it burning a heat so hot that you can feel your skin start to sweat? How hot is it, Sam? Are your panties wet with its heat? Do you need to cool down with a cube of smooth as silk ice that melts as it rubs against your burning skin? How good would that feel when shocking cold meets burning hot? How good would it feel when my cool tongue dipped through your flesh over and over again, licking the heat off of your salty skin until you're cool enough to begin heating back up again?"

There was a pause and then in a very soft commanding voice, Collins purred. "Open your eyes, Sam. I know you've closed them. The pleasure is too intense for you to keep your eyes open. The pleasure is mounting as you move your fingers. Exploring, dipping, feeling. You're squeezing your eyes shut tight, as you experience the intensity of each and every stroke. One stroke, two stroke, three…"

"Ohhh!" I groaned, clenching my teeth, opening my eyes wide in shock as the sound of a searing loud blaring of horns pierced the air, and I swerved, nearly missing the blue van in the next lane. "Collins!" I screamed.

"Sam!" Collins' voice cried through my phone. "Are you alright? Sam?"

My heart was beating so fast as the van swerved inches away from colliding with my small white compact car, and narrowly missed crushing me to bits. I gripped the handle with both hands so hard, turning to readjust the car, and within a split second, was back in my lane, breathing hard.

"Sam!" Collins' voice sounded so far away, coming through my phone on the seat next to me. My small earpiece had fallen off, and I couldn't make out all the words coming through.

The hard turn of my car had pushed the phone clear to the other side of the car, and I couldn't reach it.

Concentrate on the road. Focus, Sam. Get yourself together and calm down.

Finding You Finding Me (You & Me Trilogy #2)

I took a deep breath and slowly let out the air as I listen to my strong inner voice, the voice that would pop up when I needed to listen to what I needed to do. I took another deep breath, trying to calm myself down.

I can do this. I will get through this.

Again and again until my hands were only shaking mildly.

Finally, I was back in control. The car was driving smoothly in its own lane, as though nothing had happened. Just a few more blocks and I'll be driving into the parking lot of Sawyer House like just another day at work. Another day where my advice on the phone to any teen, young adult or adult can help make a difference in someone's life. Another day when I would get involved in the lives of other people's problems. I brought a trembling finger to my hair to push a few strands out of my face and looked in the mirror. My hazel eyes stared back at me from the mirror, as though mocking me.

Kailin Gow

When will you learn, Sam, it's time to work on your own problems...time to start saving yourself.

"Easy for you to say!" I shouted. "You have no idea how much I have to deal with. It'll be so easy to give up, so easy to leave and go far away! Leave behind all the messed up fucked up shit I have facing me and go far away to Stanford."

But no, you didn't leave, did you, Sam? You gave up that opportunity. Lost that chance to run far away from all that mess. Why?

"Because...because I know it will never end until I face it. Because I know. In me, deep inside me, I lost someone, and I need to find her again or I will always always be lost."

It hit me then what I'd given up today when I didn't mail in my response, when I pulled my envelope out of the mail lady's hands, announcing to Stanford my acceptance of the scholarship and enrollment into their accelerated psychology program. My longtime dream. The culmination of years of hard work, and my means to escape the harsh reality behind my perfect façade of a family. It hit me all at once, along with the shock of nearly losing my life within inches. I let out a wail and then the sobbing and the heaving began just when I finally pulled into an empty space and parked the car.

"Sam!" Collins' voice shouted through my phone from the other side of my car. "Oh my God, Sam! I'm so sorry…I got carried away…are you hurt? Are you alright? Oh God, I don't know what I'll do if…if…" A groan of frustration screamed through the phone, loud enough to shake me out of my state and glance over to where the phone was…my lifeline to Collins right now. "Sam," his voice sounded muffled. "Susan…I need to see you now. I can't face losing you right when I've found you again."

Susan? At the name "Susan", my head snapped back up and my back straightened, forcing me to become all business, to become practical, serious, and focused. "Susan" - my trigger word for getting me to hold everything together worked to get me to stop the uncontrollable sobbing.

Get your shit together, girl. Susan's voice of reason rang through to my brain. *You are going to stop crying, get out of the car, walk into Sawyer House, and have a great day today.*

And then face Collins, whom I haven't seen or touch in months, whom the mere sound of his voice can drive up my body temperature, and his touch would do much more than that. Considerably more. For before I met Collins that fateful day outside of my high school guidance counselor's office, I never dated, never kissed, and never wanted to feel the touch of a boy or man on me. Until I bumped into Collins, and his entire presence caused something within me to jump out and feel something again. Not only something, but a passion so deep that I craved it like air. Collins was right about something alright. He had touched a part of me that was so hidden that I didn't even know it existed. That it would take a strong person to dig through the layers I've developed over the years to find me and pull me out.

Today I had turned down my chance to start a whole new life at Stanford away from my messed up family and my messed up past, for one reason and one reason alone – there was something else here at home that I knew would be better. My subconscious self knew what it was, but I didn't. I couldn't even begin to tell. Whatever it was, though, whatever it appeared to be…somehow it all began with Collins.

Chapter 2

"My God! Sam, what happened to you?" Derek greeted me at the door with a can of Red Bull, something he's been doing since I would arrive barely awake, having only slept a few hours each night to fit in my hours at Sawyer House and finishing up the rest of my high school AP (Advanced Placement) classes, which would get me enough college credits for me to finish college a year or two earlier. He rushed over to me and folded me into his arms, hugging me tightly, while kissing the top of my head, his tall, lanky body making me feel tiny in his embrace. "You look like you've just seen a ghost."

I melted into his embrace, feeling his strong arms tighten a little more around me. My legs felt like jelly, and I realized I had a little trouble walking steadily. Did my near crash have that much of an effect on me?

Get it together, Sam! Susan, my inner voice tried smacking me.

I took a deep breath and said, "I'll be fine, Derek."

"Why do you look as pale as a ghost, and why are you shivering in my arms then?" Derek asked. "What happened, Sam?"

No use trying to hide anything from the super observant Derek. He was too well-trained to let something slip by. "Um, I nearly collided with a large car on my way here. Missed by a few inches…"

Derek immediately pulled me tighter to his chest and began rubbing my back. "Oh Sammy, you must've been so scared." He pulled back a little to look into my eyes, his brown ones searching. "How are you now?"

I smiled up at him. "I'm fine. I'm fine. Don't make such a fuss," I swatted his hand away while I tried straightening up. "I don't want the new peer counselor I'm training today to see me wimpy like this. Besides, how is the new peer counselor?"

Derek smiled, "You can never appear wimpy, Sam. Not in a million years. You're one of the strongest girls I know." His fingers reached out to tenderly touch my cheeks and then my nose. "You don't know how proud I am of you...so proud. You're graduating Valedictorian, going to be the youngest peer counselor trainer (even beating my record), and getting accepted to the Stanford psychology program. You don't have to worry about being a slacker at all. Talking about slackers...I didn't think anyone who looked like our newest peer counselor would be interested at all with Sawyer House. You're in for a challenge, but I think you'll enjoy that. I'm hoping I'm proven wrong about this guy...and that you'll be the one proving it."

"Derek, for someone who seemed so sensitive, yet so smart, I can't believe you can form quick judgments of people based on their looks."

Derek smiled a shy smile then. "I was right about you, though, Sam...a beautiful girl with brains walked into Sawyer House wanting to help people by becoming a peer counselor, and she turned out to be just that," he grinned. "And much much more."

"Gee, thanks," I said smiling, feeling better already.

Finding You Finding Me (You & Me Trilogy #2)

"And you know what?" Derek asked, pulling me to him urgently now and encircling me in a friendlier embrace. His lips touched my forehead and then it moved down to the tip of my nose until they brushed against my lips. He pressed into my lips until it was open and then his tongue lightly touched mine. "You're much more than I ever dreamed of when we first met. Much more, Sam. I know you wanted only friendship, but you know how I feel about you."

He grabbed my hand and led me quickly into the private conference room where he leaned me up against the wall and kissed me again, this time more hungrily. "Sam," he kissed me harder with each word he uttered. "Sam, my Sam," his kisses were now desperate and all over my face, my neck. "God, I'm so grateful you didn't get hit by that car. You've come to mean so much to me, Sam, and if I lost you..." he stopped kissing me for a second. "I don't know what I'd do."

"Derek...I'm fine. I'm safe. Don't worry about me, please." I tried to pull away, but his hand held me in place against the wall.

"But I do, Sam. I can't help it. These past few weeks when you've come in almost everyday to work, and when you would hang out with me at my college dorm at UC Irvine, experiencing the life of a college student with me...has meant so much to me. I've loved every minute of it. And, Sam..." Derek hesitated. "You and Collins McGregor are no longer together. You haven't been for months...so maybe it's time to move on...time for you to give someone else a chance..."

I stared at Derek as his face flushed, making the air between us grow thick. "Derek...I...Collins...there's something you should know..."

Derek was about to say something when his eyes went from my face to an area to my left behind me. Then as though right on cue, there was a knock on the door before it opened and a tall, but muscular, shaggy-haired sandy blond teen boy about fifteen or sixteen years old walked in. His hair was down to his shoulders, and from what I could see of his face, now covered by his long bangs, he had piercings all over his face...his eyebrow, his nostril, and his lips. Dressed in a thin black and white skull and crossbones t-shirt over black too-long denim jeans and black hi-tops, the boy looked more like a skater than anything.

"Um, Derek?" he said, his voice raspy as though he had smoked way too many cigarettes over his young years. "I've poured over the scripts, and sat with a few of the counselors during their calls. I think I got the hang of it for now. But, what I want to know, is…when do I get to sit and be trained by Susan?"

At the mention of my call center name Susan, my interest in this strange skater boy with piercings increased. I was already intrigued by his appearance, but when he brought up his eagerness to be trained by Susan, I took a closer look at him. Did I know him? Was he one of the callers I've talked to as Susan? Why did he seem so eager to be trained by me? Why not Derek, the head trainer?

"Hi," I said, extending my hand out for a shake. "I'm Susan."

The boy flipped his bangs out of his face, and I could see his icy blue eyes assess me indifferently at first, and then as his eyes went up my legs, my waist, my breasts, and then my face, it changed from indifference to intense interest and finally to desire. "Hi, Susan," he said grinning, "So you're Susan." He seemed to sigh as he put his image of me along with what he expected, together. "You are definitely a lot prettier and younger than I expected…just your voice…" he stammered.

"Thank you," I said. "I didn't know you know of Susan. It's the name I use here so everything is anonymous. They try to discourage outside contacts between counselors and callers, and adopting a name other than your own seem to help that cause." I nearly wink, as though that was an inside joke. "Do you have one already or did Derek neglect to tell you that?"

The pierced boy laughed, looking at Derek. "Yes, Derek did make it a point to get me to adopt a counselor name."

"So, what is it?" I smiled. Might as well make this pierced boy get used to me being in charge of his training so he is properly trained.

"Billy," the boy said. "The name's Billy."

My smile faded. As much as Susan was the trigger word for helping my self-controlled self take over, the name Billy was enough of a word to get my stomach turn involuntarily into a combination of strong fear, disgust, and anger. I looked closely at Billy's good-looking face, trying to see if he resembled someone I knew with the same name, and couldn't find any similarities. However, something about Billy seemed familiar, but I couldn't put my hand on it quite yet.

Chapter 3

Billy looked confused for a moment. "Did I say something wrong or do something to upset you, Susan?"

"Um, no," I said. "I'm just curious why you chose the name Billy."

We had sat down at my desk and I was sitting where normally Derek would sit, to the side of Billy.

"Does it mean anything to you?" Billy asked, assessing me with his cool blue eyes. They unnerved me, as though he knew me, knew all about what happened to me when I was younger, all my deep dark secrets.

"No," I shook my head. "It means nothing to me." Billy looked a little disappointed then, but he said cheerily. "So what kinds of calls do you get Susan?"

"The usual," I said. "Cliques, bullying, drug use, dating, image, and abuse."

"Anything really different?" Billy asked.

"Like what?" I asked, not sure where Billy was heading with his questions.

"Guys who just want to talk to someone, a pretty girl who they can fantasize about?"

Billy was staring at me with a mischievous look. If he was a character from some fantasy book, I'd say he reminded me of a prankster fairy.

"And, you'd think these teenage boys would be calling the center to get their high on that? Why not call a sex line or something?"

"Because," Billy said smiling, as though he was hiding a funny joke from me, "it costs them money to talk to those phone sex lines while here…you have such a sexy and seductive voice, Susan…"

I shot up from my seat then and pulled "Billy" out of my seat, grabbed him by his collar and leaned into his face to look him in the eye. "I don't know what kind of prank you're trying to pull here, but at Sawyer House, we take everyone's calls pretty seriously. If you are here to make a joke out of what we do, then you can pack your stuff and just leave right now."

"Oh, don't get so hot and bothered, Susan," Billy laughed. "I don't do that, but I know of a group of guys who did, and are planning to."

"What do you mean?" I asked, narrowing my eyes at his twinkling blue ones. I wanted to slap that mirth out of him and set him straight.

"You're quite a hottie, Susan," Billy said, licking his lips and looking me up and down.

Now I was seething mad. "I don't know who put you up to this, but I want no part of it. Tell your friends to go fuck off, and if I find any one of them trying to pull a prank on me or anyone from Sawyer House, believe me, you'll find more than the police on your tail." I grabbed his backpack, his jacket, and him, and pushed him towards the exit of the building. "Go before I tell Gail why you're really here!"

"Slut," he said.

"Charming," I said. "Bet that gets you the girls all the time." He turned towards me to face me again right before I slammed the door in his face.

I wasn't finished yet and walked over to Derek's desk where he was talking to one of the new peer counselors. I pulled him aside and crossed my arms.

"Derek, your instinct was right on about Billy."

Derek's face immediately became concerned. "Where is he? What happened?"

I sighed, not wanting to bring up this heavy topic, but said, "I kicked him out."

"What?" Derek exclaimed. "What did he do?"

I shook my head. "He's not here to become a peer counselor, Derek."

"I don't understand," Derek said. "He came highly-recommended. A friend of Gail's recommended him, and said he would make a great peer counselor. Been through a lot of things himself, even went through therapy, so he can relate well with anyone who calls in."

"Derek," I said firmly. "Billy may seem like a great candidate for a peer counselor, but he wasn't here for that apparently. He made everything we do here sound trivial, like it was a big joke!"

"Why would he do that?" Derek asked.

"Beats me," I said. "He said my voice was seductive and guys would be calling Sawyer House just to get phone sex from me or any of the girls who volunteered as counselors here. He also called me 'slut'," when I kicked him out the door."

Derek was fuming mad now. "That jerk," he said. "I don't care if he's Gail's best friend or relative, but that is no way to talk to you." Derek bunched his fists together and looked like he wanted to head straight out to confront Billy. "Stay here," Derek said, while starting to head out to the parking lot. "I've got some words for him that…"

"Derek," I said, wanting this whole incident to be over. "I think he's gone already. Just let it go."

"But," Derek said, "how dare he talk to you like that? How dare he tried to put you down. I should have listened to my instincts about him first before unleashing him on you." He shook his head. "He was going to be the perfect recruit, a peer counselor close in age to our callers, yet experienced enough to have gone through the same experiences as the callers. I'll just have to let Gail know it didn't work out."

"I'll do it instead," I said. "If you don't want to face her on this. I'm the one who discovered what Billy was up to. Witnessed it, too, so it makes sense for me to tell Gail."

"If you're up for it," Derek said. "I'll go in to talk to Gail with you, if you want."

I smiled then. "I'd like that, Derek, but I think it's probably better for me to talk to her alone." With that, I turned around away from Derek and was about to head over to Gail's office when I felt a light but firm tap on the shoulder from behind.

I thought it was Derek, turning around to tell him I'll be fine. "Like I said, Derek…" I began, but realized the large muscular man dressed in black who stood imposingly right behind me was not Derek.

It was Vincent, the loyal and reliable driver who worked for Collins.

I couldn't help giving him a welcome back hug and then pulling back. "If you'll come with me, Miss Sullivan," he said, "Mr. McGregor wants to see you now."

Chapter 4

I turned to go grab my purse from my desk when Vincent gently placed his gigantic right hand on my shoulders, stopping me in place.

"But I have to get my purse and clock out and…"

"Already taken care of," Vincent said, handing me my purse and soft pink sweater.

"I still have to talk to Gail about something and to let Derek know I'm leaving early," I said.

Vincent didn't blink, but touched my shoulders again, turning me around to face the direction of Gail's office. I blinked, not believing what I was seeing.

Walking out of her office, in deep conversation with Gail, in contrast to her dark blunt bobbed haircut, small frame and soft grey sweater dress, was a tall, long-legged and lean, but muscular young man in his mid-twenties. Blond with icy blue eyes, sculpted cheekbones and full sensual lips, Collins McGregor looked as beautifully flawless as the day I bumped headfirst into him at school.

He was dressed in a black Armani suit with a silk grey and red striped tie. Impeccable, but sexy at the same time, as the first button of his shirt was unbuttoned, revealing a hint of his smooth golden tanned skin underneath. Immediately my mind turned to the delicious image of Collins without his shirt on as I remembered all too fondly.

My breath almost catch when he stopped talking to Gail, turned, and faced me. It was as though the world stood still as his icy blue eyes fringed with dark lashes cut clear across the room to focus on mine. It's been months since I've seen him, touched him. Months since we've tasted each other.

But as soon as we've laid eyes on one another, it was as though we've never left each other. I saw him take a breath as we stared at each other, his eyes never leaving mine. I must have inhaled deeply at the same time because I didn't realize I was holding my breath until Collins appeared before me, taking me into his arms and enfolded me tightly to his chest.

"Sam," he whispered into my ears. He held me for a while more before he abruptly pulled away from me. "Thank God you look alright." He looked me up and down, his eyes burning as he perused every inch of me. "Now, if we can get you out of here and to someplace where we can be alone, I'll be able to check you out further to see how you really are."

I could see the worry in his face give way to another feeling immediately as his lips curled slightly at the corners into a wicked sexy smile. "Let's start with dinner, and then we can have dessert. But first..." he led me to where Gail stood at her door, watching us.

"Gail," he said respectfully, "I'm taking Sam out for dinner, and if you need her tonight..."

Gail shook her head. "Nah, you go and take the night off. Sam deserves a break once in a while, and I'm just glad to see how happy she looks right now."

I looked happy? I wasn't sure about that, as confused as I was looking into Collins' beautiful blue eyes, and filled with reservations.

"It'll do Mr. McGregor some good, too," Gail said before she nodded and headed back into her office.

My eyes followed her retreating back until she was out of sight, and then I looked questioningly at Collins. What did Gail know about Collins to make her say that?

Collins smiled a big Cheshire Cat smile that made my heart thump loudly in my ears. It was boyish, sexy, and adorable at the same time. He took my hand and brought it up to his lips, kissing the knuckles. "Whatever Gail recommends, I won't refute her," he said with a grin.

I cocked my eyebrows and tilted my head to look at Collins more carefully. There was nothing there on him…no substance, no magic, nothing but just Collins' sexy charm. Even if he just met Gail, I was sure he would have charmed the pants off of her, but something told me he and Gail did not just meet. Maybe they knew each other and Gail was so encouraging and nice to him because of the scholarship he donated to Sawyer House a while back. Maybe Gail knew of Collins because he was in all the society magazines as the most eligible bachelor, and she used to know people in that circle because of her private practice as a psychiatrist. Whatever it was, I was curious, but I didn't have the time to get into it as Vincent swept Collins and me quickly out of Sawyer House and into Collins' long black limo with the privacy panel separating Vincent from the backseat where Collins sat next to me.

As soon as we were seated and Vincent had started the limo, moving it smoothly through traffic, Collins pulled me into his lap, reaching out to cup my face in his large hands before his mouth crushed down onto mine in a searingly hungry kiss. My mouth responded to his, kiss for kiss, starving to taste every inch of his mouth.

When our tongues touched, I felt myself moan and press closer to him, wanting to shift my position so that my rear end wasn't bumping up and rubbing against his hard arousal.

"Sam," he groaned, as I shifted again, brushing against him as I turn to sit facing him, my legs now straddling him, "I missed this, I miss you so much, but if you don't stop squirming against me, rubbing against me like that, I don't think we can make it to dinner."

I kissed him and said, "do we have to eat dinner?"

Finding You Finding Me (You & Me Trilogy #2)

Collins laughed then, a deep velvety laugh that made my stomach flip. Even his laugh made me want him more. "No, we have to go to this dinner. I made a promise."

A promise? I pulled my mouth away from his for a while and looked up at him, my eyes questioning him.

His eyes looked into mine, softening and then filled with a look of adoration. "Baby," he said, "Don't worry about it. It's a promise I made to the person we're meeting."

"We have company?" I asked. When did Collins ever take me out for dinner to meet with other people?

"Yes," Collins said. "In order for me and you to work, in order for us to really have a functioning relationship, Sam, we'll have to do this."

I took a deep breath and exhaled. Before this moment, when it came to Collins McGregor, I had only thought with my wanton irrational side, my Lola, as I called her. She was the one who made me toss caution to the wind and jump head first questions later into my forbidden relationship with billionaire bad boy Collins McGregor, as scandalizing as it seemed for the chaste virginal Pastor's daughter to carrying on a relationship with one of America's most eligible and most rumored about billionaire bachelor.

Collins kissed me on the temple and sat me down next to him, readjusting the front of his pants. "As much as I want to go through with what we started right here until we're both naked, sweaty, and pounding each other in every which way space will permit in this backseat; we have to stop."

I blushed, thinking of the very image he painted just now, and gulped, wondering if it was possible to do some of the things I've seen him do in his tapes, within the space of the backseat. Just remembering how he looked when he was writhing in ecstasy and how his face looked as he found his release, made my mouth watered as I stared at his lips, his mouth, and his eyes. "Collins," I whispered hoarsely, "I'm not prepared to meet someone for dinner right now, not the way I'm dressed, and especially not the way I feel…"

"You're dressed fine, and believe me, the person we're meeting wouldn't mind knowing how you're feeling right now."

I gulped. I knew Collins was into certain kinds of alternative or even kinky acts, but I didn't think he would bring someone else into it. "Um, Collins, I'm not sure…"

His large hands slipped up my thighs and started kneading my skin in a luxuriously slow circle, dangerously close to my inner thigh. Inches from where my body was heated up, waiting for his touch. "Relax," Collins said softly, barely a whisper. "It's just a dinner meeting, and afterwards, we'll see what comes of it."

"But," I started to protest. "I just want to be with you. You alone. I've waited so long to see you again, and I even," I took a deep breath. I couldn't believe I felt so emotional about this, so young and naïve. Didn't I know what I was getting into when it came to Collins McGregor and his dark needs?

Collins smiled widely then and he leaned over to tenderly kiss me on the lips. "You will," he said. He squeezed my thigh then and beamed. "I'm proud of your progress, Sam. Months ago, you wouldn't even admit to wanting to be touched, you wouldn't even want me to undress you completely. Now…"

I blushed, looking down, and acknowledging the truth with what he said. I couldn't get past a certain point in our relationship without breaking down into traumatizing paralyzing fear. Now… "It's because I've watched you," I said. "In your tapes. I've seen what you've done and are capable of doing. I can anticipate it, Collins. In some strange bizarre way, because I know and can expect what is your next move, for some reason, it makes me…um…not scared." I can feel my face burning red and my ears heating up. "I want to experience those same things with you, Collins. I've never wanted anything more."

Collins' palm gently touched my cheeks, and when I turned my face up to look at him, I can see tears in his eyes. "Sam," he said. "You don't know how much this means to me." He cupped my face in both his hands and planted kisses on my lips, my cheeks, my eyelids, and my forehead. "My Sammy, my girl…I thought I lost you, were losing you when we came so close to becoming more, but thank goodness, I was wrong." He kissed me fully on the lips again, and this time, I can feel my cheeks wet, as his hot mouth devoured mine. When he pulled back, I thought it was his tears I was feeling against my cheeks, but realized when I can see his face more clearly and how dry his cheeks looked, that the tears I thought were his, had really been my own.

Kailin Gow

Chapter 5

"It didn't take long for us to reach where we were going for dinner. Vincent pulled up to the entrance of a tall modern glass and steel building located about 20 minutes from Sawyer House, and came around to open my door.

Collins joined me, took my arm, and walked me to the double glass doors leading into the building. The lobby had an impressive water garden, but other than that, it appeared to be occupied by professional offices, not restaurants.

"Collins," I said, "where's the restaurant?"

Collins licked his lips nervously and said, "Um, actually, we're not here for the restaurant."

I stopped walking and stood facing him. "Then where are we going?"

"Remember I said we needed to meet someone in order for us to have this relationship? In order to try to make it work?"

"I thought we were meeting them for dinner," I said.

"We were, we are, but first, we have to meet them here."

"Why?" I asked.

Collins let out an exasperated breath and said, "You sure have a lot of questions all of a sudden, Sweetie." He pulled me in and kissed me on the lips, a soft, but firm reassuring kiss that hinted at something a lot sexier and wild to come. "Just trust me, Sam, meeting this person before dinner, will be worth it."

"Worth it, huh?" I teased, stepping up to him and nearly plastering myself to him.

There were a few people in the lobby, but I didn't care. If Collins wanted to play some kind of game with me, then I'll play it right back at him. If he wanted to be secretive about this whole thing, especially when it came to something involving us, then I can keep things from him, too.

"Sam," Collins said, peeling my arms off of his shoulders and setting me chastely in front of him so he can lead me to the elevators. "I don't want to keep anything from you, but under the circumstances, this has to be an as-you-know situation. And it's nothing to worry about." He kissed my forehead again and said against my cheeks, "Please, Sam, trust me. I need to get your trust on this. I need to know that you can have some kind of faith in me and our relationship."

Collins was serious then, and his beautiful blue eyes held my hazel ones, directly and intensely, strong, but pleadingly soft at once. My heart went out to him, seeing how he was suddenly so nervous, he was uncharacteristically quiet. He licked his lips again, and I realized he was waiting for me to make the first move.

I gently reached out for his hand and held onto it with mine and said, "Come on, then. Don't want to keep our guest waiting."

Collins nodded, leading me to the elevators.

Finding You Finding Me (You & Me Trilogy #2)

Once inside the elevator, Collins pressed the button for the top floor. We stared at each other as the elevator door closed, noting that there was no one else in the elevator besides us. We still had our hands together, and as soon as the doors closed, Collins' hands left mine and traveled to the back of my waist. With one single lift, he had me against the wall of the elevator, my legs straddled around his waist before he crashed his mouth hungrily over mine. His hands roamed around my back, while he held me in place with his weight, and stroked my tongue with his. His need for me was so intense, and my need to have him fill me, made me tighten my legs around him while I tried to untie his tie and unbutton his white shirt.

I wanted to open up his shirt and kiss the beautifully golden warm skin of his throat and then his smooth bare chest. I wanted to run my hands all over his muscular chest and down to his rock hard abs, down his pelvic V, and further so I can feel how much he wanted me. Pressed against me so tightly against the wall, I could feel him, pulsing against me, enlarged with need. "Sam," he breathed into my mouth. "I want to fuck you so badly, I'm thinking of holding off on this meeting."

"Hmmm," I said, still kissing his lips and then sucking hard on his tongue. It was instinctual, and I just knew I wanted to taste him and please him in any and every physical way I could offer.

I continued sucking on his tongue until he groaned, and nearly dropped me as a shiver went through both of us. "What. Do. You. Want?" he said between heavy panting and kissing.

"Don't we have to meet them in order to move forward?" I asked coyly, my mind consumed with all thoughts of how to get Collins' shirt and pants off, rather than talk about meetings and appointments.

"Yes," Collins said. "We have to, but I get the feeling…" He hesitated for a while before slamming down his head into my chest and began kissing the top of my breasts at my cleavage. His hand snaked in underneath my shirt and lifted my bra up so that now his fingers were rubbing my nipples back and forth.

"Collins," I purred, almost losing it. "When did we have to meet…"

Finding You Finding Me (You & Me Trilogy #2)

I stopped as he lifted up my shirt, baring my breasts to the air, and tugged one of my breasts into his mouth where he used his tongue to nip and lick my sensitive nipples into full peakness. When he finished taking one breast to its full apex of sensations, he hungrily latched onto the other, sucking and licking until I would explode.

"Collins," I cried. "We have to stop or I'll want to go all the way." I tugged frantically at the belt holding his pants together, and then the zipper. I wanted to feel his warmth in me so badly now, I didn't care if I was tearing at his clothes.

"I love this animalistic go-all-out side of you, Sammy," he growled. "I knew underneath that prim and proper good girl was this tigress who's insatiable."

"Guess I can imagine more of what I want to do with you now that my eyes are open to the possibilities," I said. "And right now, I want you to feel me, to relieve me, Collins."

"Oh," Collins smiled. "I'll do more than that to you, Sammy. I'll…" with one fell swoop, he reached under my skirt and tore off my panties. He took a look at it, and looked a little disappointed. "Not the ones with the heart on it that I so loved," he said. "But I guess that's a good thing because it means I didn't tear that one apart." He placed my torn panties into his pocket and proceeded to bring his hand up my thighs and then directly rubbing and touching my most sensitive parts with his fingers.

He had me writhing against the wall, wanting to pull him closer. "I see I've been neglectful in my duties," Collins said seductively. "Some of you need a bit more attention than just that." He lifted me higher now as though I was as light as a pillow, and held me with both hands around my waist, arms extended up, and then he lowered me, naked, wet, and hot for him directly in front of his mouth until I was sitting on his shoulders. "Umm," he said, "maybe we can skip dinner after all and go straight to dessert." With that, I felt his wet tongue begin working on me stroke after blissful slow stroke.

I was so on the verge of exploding when I felt his tongue reached all the way in, sliding deep in and then out and back in repeatedly until I began clenching. The sensation was searingly hot and cool at the same time, I began shaking hard, uncontrollably and deliciously until I felt almost spent. When my tremors subsided, Collins lowered my body down until he was facing me, and then he hungrily kissed my mouth, as though he was starving and couldn't get enough.

"That was so beautiful, Sam," he said. "So fucking deliciously beautiful." He kissed me one last hard time, and then pulled back before he pulled me into a tight hug. "Sam, you've just had an orgasm." He kissed me on the lips, gently now. "And I see many more to come…"

He took out a handkerchief and folded it into a nice rectangle before he wiped between my legs, cleaning me up, and then placed it back into his pocket. "If we had done this at my place, Sammy, I'd strip you and wash every part of you in the shower. I'd wash your beautiful smooth skin, and shampoo your gorgeous thick dark hair. Afterwards, I'd rub scented oils all over you, and then take you to our bed where we begin getting you hot and exploding once again."

The image of that made me shiver all over. But there wasn't time for another release.

When the elevator reached one floor below where we were heading, I quickly adjusted my clothes and fixed my hair, while Collins buttoned up his shirt and fixed his tie. I was ready, but Collins' pants were still unzipped, unbuttoned, and unbelted. I immediately helped him there, zipping up his zipper, then buttoning it before belting it. I was very conscious of the large bulge in his pants, and I looked up at him, questioningly. "I want to reciprocate," I said. "I want to make you feel as good and fulfilled as I feel right now." I licked my lips nervously but eagerly. I have never done this before, but I was willing, driven by intense desire for him, wanting to experience everything with him.

Collins smiled, and inhaled. "The thought of you trying, just made this so much harder, but Sam…we're not doing this today. You're not ready yet, and we don't have time. We'll be lucky to be able to make it to our meeting on time now."

The elevator door stopped, and it opened up. Collins took me by the elbows and walked a little over pass the elevator and to one of the doors in the hallway. We stopped, and Collins knocked on the door, right when I noticed there was a nameplate with a name that looked very familiar to me. I blinked, not believing the name I saw on there.

"Here we are," Collins said, before the door opened, revealing the familiar face of someone I knew well.

I couldn't help dropping my mouth open.

Standing in front of us, gesturing for us to come in, was Gail herself, and it looked as though she had just come straight from Sawyer House.

Chapter 6

"Gail?" I asked, obviously surprised. I looked over at Collins and raised my eyebrows. Is this the person we're supposed to meet before dinner?

Gail laughed, and looked over at Collins. "I told you she'll react this way."

Collins nervously bit his lips, and I could see how intensely uncomfortable he had become.

"Come in, Sam and Collins," Gail said, taking my arm and maneuvering us inside the office, overlooking the city lights of Newport and with a view out to the Pacific Ocean. It was a far cry from her office at Sawyer House. "Come and make yourself comfortable," she said.

"Gail," I said, "Why are you here? What am I doing here?"

Finding You Finding Me (You & Me Trilogy #2)

Gail looked over at Collins and said, "I wished I could have told you earlier, but I'm under client/patient privileges and I can't divulge any of this as well as the fact that I knew Collins until I've gotten permission. You see... I've been Collins' psychiatrist for years, even before I stopped being in private practice and opened Sawyer House. He's one of my longest clients." She smiled and looked affectionately at Collins. "One of my celebrity clients I had when I had an office in Beverly Hills. Now all my time is at Sawyer House, except for Collins, who retained me and set me up nicely here near his offices."

I looked incredulously over at Collins and then at Gail. Why didn't Collins tell me that?

"I know Collins had started calling Sawyer House as a caller a while back when he couldn't get a hold of me and thought I was there. He was going through a challenge, a new situation, and needed to talk to someone fast about it. I wasn't there so he found himself assuming a name so that he can talk to one of the peer counselors. Well...when I called Collins back, he told me that he didn't need to talk to me, but that he thinks he can handle this new challenge on his own, and if he needed some help, he's found one of the counselors to be very helpful." Gail smiled then. "Of course, I knew it was you, Sam."

"You did?" I asked. "But, I didn't know Collins was actually…"

"I know, Sam. I know all about it. Collins didn't realized Susan was you either at first, and vice versa so…the rule at Sawyer House about a peer counselor seeing one of the callers, well, in your case, it seems you didn't know about each other's true identity, and besides, you were already seeing each other before the call. If it wasn't for those circumstances, Sam and Collins, I wouldn't allow for you two to get together. It would compromise Sawyer House's position. But, as it was a completely different case, and I know Collins' history, and I sorta have a hint of yours, Sam (Derek filled me in with everything he knew because he was concerned with what happened the first time you had a breakdown), this is different."

I nodded as my slight panic subsided. I was not here because I was in trouble with Gail or Sawyer House for having had a relationship with Collins outside of Sawyer

House. I was not going to lose my position there. And Collins…the fact that he knew Gail, but in a very discreet way since she was his psychiatrist or therapist, although I was hurt he never told me about Gail, I could understand why. "I'm sorry," I said. "If I had done anything that would have jeopardized Sawyer House's reputation…I…"

"Don't apologize, Sam," Gail said. "It's an interesting case, and frankly, I'm very fond of both of you that I think something like this can be overlooked. But as I said, you and Collins are unique circumstances, that falls outside of our usual rules. Collins has even assured me that he is no longer calling as the caller, and will be handling his challenges openly and directly with the person he has those challenges with." She looked directly into my eyes when she said "person" and the enormity of that sank in. My heart did a flip at that moment, and I felt my ears burning. I was that person Collins was going to openly and honestly work with to overcome his challenges.

I looked over at Collins, and I can see the fear, the uncertainty in his eyes. My heart went out to his then. Daggers. My Daggers have come out clean. He was trying

Kailin Gow

so hard to overcome his past…even bringing me here to meet with Gail right now. How can I say "no" to helping him?

I turned to Collins and took his hand, rubbing my thumb over his palm, trying to soothe him, trying to reassure him. Despite his stoic expression, I can feel his hand shake slightly. I knew him so well. I knew he was scared. Scared to take this step. The only way he could have a relationship with a woman was a physical one. If there was going to be anything beyond that, it would come with some conditions. In Collins' past, those conditions have always been harsh and abusive. When he reached out to me at Sawyer House, under the guise of someone else, I've learned so much about the abuse he'd faced with women in the past, starting at age thirteen when his mother prostituted him to older women to get money for her drug habit, then when he ran away and began living on the streets, he said he did things he wasn't proud of. Then came the so-called loving relationships he'd had with women who would only abuse him through their words and then physically. And the tapes…

- 63 -

Finding You Finding Me (You & Me Trilogy #2)

I should run. I should turn around and leave. What was an innocent virginal Pastor's daughter with a traumatic past of my own doing with someone so worldly, so damaged as Collins McGregor? How can I help someone like him? How? What can I do?

"Sam and Collins," Gail said. "I see both of you hesitating about this, but I'll let you know as honestly as I can, not only as a therapist, but also as a friend of you both, I think, despite the outside differences you have, you two are very similar. You two happen to care for one another very much, too. The time you've spent away from each other didn't diminish your feelings for each other, but it seems as though it brought you two closer. Sam, you've seen a part of Collins that he was terrified to show you, scared that you'll run. But you haven't. He's laid out everything about him for you, Sam, including the most intimate of all secrets…his past, his shame, and everything. He's given you a choice to run or to accept him as who he is, Sam."

Gail took a deep breath and sat down at her desk, looking down at her hands. "I was so sure you'd take the million dollars and high-tail it out to Stanford, where you can start all over, but…" she paused. "You didn't. You surprised us all, Sam. Despite how much you have set your heart on going to Stanford, you chose this. You chose not to run away. Do you know why?"

I looked at Collins' hands, which I was holding tightly. His beautiful blue eyes looked intensely at mine, intense, but soft, and full of love. There was no question about it. I loved this man. And I would do whatever it takes to help him overcome his demons. Anything.

"I stayed," I said, looking from Collins to Gail and back to Collins, "because I love Collins, and I'd do anything to help him."

Gail smiled a secret smile that reminded me of Mona Lisa. "That's what I suspected," she said. "And of course, from everything I know of you, Sam, Collins couldn't have fallen in love with anyone more perfect for him than you."

Collins spoke up then after being silent the entire time. "But will Sam be alright through all this?" he asked. "Will it be too much for her…all my needs and…"

Finding You Finding Me (You & Me Trilogy #2)

"It's up to Sam," Gail said. "She's her own person, and she's an adult. She may have had something traumatic that happened to her that she's working through herself, but it isn't her fault, and she is and will be strong enough to overcome it."

"But my needs are so intense, and she's still so vulnerable, young, and innocent," Collins said. "I don't care about my therapy as much as it is to help her, Gail. Will her being with me cause her any harm?"

"I don't think you can hurt her, Collins," Gail said. "You have issues, but you're not a monster, Collins. You can never hurt the woman you love."

"But I'm not normal," Collins said. "I'm a deviant, I…"

Gail stood up and walked over to us, turning Collins to face her. "No, you are not a deviant, Collins. You are normal. You have some hiccups along the way to being just like everyone else, but every experience you've had, good or bad, has shaped you into the sensitive, strong, resilient, and caring man that you are today."

"Will you help us?" Collins asked with tears in his eyes. "Will you help me be the man worthy of Sam's love?"

"I'll try to step in whenever you need me," Gail said. "But the most important person you should be discussing your relationship with is the woman you want to be with...Sam, and for her to be open and honest with you, too. For your relationship to work, you have to let each other know your boundaries and expectations. You'll have to learn to trust each other. Both of you have issues in the past that will come up and become barriers for you to overcome, but fate or destiny has thrown you two together. I have a hunch if you love each other enough, you'll overcome those barriers, and you'll do it together."

Collins pulled Gail into his chest for a big bear hug then. His cheeks were wet with tears, and he was telling her, that he thought everything was so hopeless a few months ago when he left for Europe and left me behind, that he thought he would never find love or be able to have a normal relationship. But now, he's never been so happy for this chance. "And I will do everything I can," he said to me, pulling me in for the group hug, "to keep you."

Chapter 7

We had dinner afterwards. Collins, Gail, and I in a restaurant nearby where we had our own private room. It felt strange having Gail, whom I saw as my mentor at Sawyer House, act as my therapist, too, or rather, Collins' therapist. I felt self-conscious at first around her, knowing what she knew about Collins and me, and also what she knew about us. Collins had told her about our incredibly hot ride up the elevator to her office and how I had reached an orgasm. My face was flaming red when she nodded, pleased with what he was telling her.

"That's amazing progress," she said to Collins and to me. "You're so close to being comfortable with your intimacy." She looked very pleased. "Given your past,

Collins, I would say you have made enormous progress to get to this point."

"I was tempted," Collins said. "A couple of times, but with Sam/Susan, I tried to stay in control."

Mortified, I kept staring down at my hands. I wasn't used to discussing my sex life in front of people, let alone my boss. But Gail was different. She wasn't just my boss, but a highly-trained respected psychiatrist. "Good, good," Gail said. "Sam, for you to reach the point of orgasm that you did, for you to get beyond your fears of intimacy and touch, you've come a long ways as well."

"All I wanted to do was to be there for him," I said. "I didn't even think of myself. I was focused on him, and with that, I wasn't afraid."

"Well, that's what I thought would happen, only you've pushed through that fear very quickly. And in the heat of the moment," Gail said. "What I wish for both of you is to be able to have that and more, all the time, in the heat of the moment and in any normal situation." Gail took out a sheet of paper and began writing. "Look, I know you both want to speed this along, and I would love for you to, but we really have to take it one step at a time so it's not too much and you end up regressing...which could be worse."

Collins took a sip of water and calmly said, "What do you suggest we do?"

"Don't live together for now. I know you want to have Sam live with you, like before, but that's a bit soon. She needs to have a place of her own. You need to have that boundary."

I spoke up, realizing this is what I wanted all along. "I was planning on moving out of my parents' place and getting a place, an apartment of my own near UC Irvine's campus."

"I'll help you find one," Collins said, without skipping a beat.

"There you go," Gail said, pleased with how easily Collins and I agreed with what she suggested.

Later on, when Collins left to go take a phone call, leaving Gail and I alone at the table, Gail took my hands in hers and squeezed it. "Sam," she said. "I know everyone is expecting me to tell you to back off from this relationship with a man like Collins. I know how much your father will disapprove of the advice I'm giving you. I know all the parents in the world will be saying that I should tell you to stay a virgin, be chaste and all that. But I'm not the moral police, and I'm not here to tell you to remain a virgin or to stay a "good girl" whatever that means or to be wary of guys like Collins. You know all that already, and you don't need me to tell you any of it. What I'm telling you is advice from experience with the choices you've already made. You've made the choice to see and be with Collins, to have a relationship with him, and him with you. You're young, but you're also an adult so I can't shelter you. I can arm you with advice to help you make grown-up decisions and to help you have the most satisfying and happy relationship you can with the person you choose to be with."

She smiled, still clasping my hands in hers. "I know it was shocking to see me in this role, as Collins McGregor's therapist. Normally you wouldn't even know, except he gave me permission to tell you and to bring you into his sessions with me. He's also asked me to work with you." She became very gentle as she said, "I know you're carrying a big burden, a big guilt right now that stems from something in your past, and it can get in the way of you having a fulfilling relationship. It can even get to the point where you're so debilitated from functioning that you shut down."

"I was…I was, that one time when Derek found me, I was going through so much," I said.

"Yes, you were, but it was also because of something triggered by Collins or by something Collins represent. Fear of intimacy, some kind of shame, guilt…am I right, Sam?"

I thought back to just today at Sawyer House. I had felt this panic, the sudden tightening in my stomach, the dread and then the fear earlier today. It wasn't just the training gone wrong of the prank trainer/stalker Billy, if that was his name. It was the name Billy, whom I have such a strongly negative association, it generated a sickly physical response in me, just hearing his name. Obviously, despite my training as a peer counselor, despite how much I knew about psychology, I still was not over the Billy incident from when I was thirteen or fourteen and harassed so badly by a bully that I was nearly raped by him.

But that wasn't all. It was the way everyone treated me afterwards that forever made me feel damaged, dirty, and unworthy so much so that I've spent my entire life afterwards, working hard to try to win everyone's acceptance again. I worked so hard to be the good girl, to be the perfect daughter, and to be what everyone expected of me...in the end, or at least right now in the present, what I realized was that all that didn't matter. It's the one who stick with you through thick and thin who matter, and that had been people like Gail, Derek, and Collins.

I finally answered Gail back. "Yes," I said. "It was, it is. And you're right. I can't do this alone."

Gail's hand squeezed mine again. "You're not, Sam. You're never alone. I know you have issues of your own that you haven't dealt with...if you need to talk about that, feel free to just come into my office, and we can."

"Thanks," I said, trying not to think about my issues. "I'll take you up on your offer for sure."

Chapter 8

The next couple of days, I began packing, ready to move out of the cozy cottage-style Newport Beach house I've lived in for the past four years since we've moved to the Orange Coast of Southern California. Originally a run-down fixer upper older cottage beach house on the cliff with a view of the ocean, my parents had lovingly remodeled it to the sweet little cottage house with a white picket fence that it now was.

Although I loved the house, I couldn't live there any longer knowing how my father felt about me, with me finding out that I was not his child after all, but some result of an one-night stand my mother had when she was barely twenty, fresh from the wild country of Texas, with hopes and dreams of making it in Hollywood...only to be knocked up by the first gorgeous guy who showed her attention and was nice to her - my so-called real dad who probably didn't even know that I existed. And the man who I thought was my father, the boy who became a pastor and married the seemingly innocent pretty girl from Texas, the man whom I grew up with, practically avoided me and my mother the last couple of months since I found out.

He wasn't here this Saturday morning as he was at church preparing for a Spring retreat. For married couples, go figure. As much of a mess that was our family life at home with my parents' impending divorce and my mother's drinking problem, which she swore she was managing because of her AA classes, what never failed about them, about us, was the perfect façade we managed to put out there for the congregation. We were always on our best behavior when we were at my father's church – the handsome charismatic pastor with his beautiful wife and daughters. Mom ran events and put together ladies' socials including book clubs, while I played the piano during sermons or helped out at the youth center with Pastor Michael, a young handsome pastor fresh from missionary trips to Asia and South America.

Finding You Finding Me (You & Me Trilogy #2)

For all it's worth, despite the hot mess at my parent's home (funny how I refer to this cottage house I've lived in for years as their home now instead of mine), I somehow did not walk away from it all, as I had originally planned months ago before meeting Collins. Instead of packing to move upper north to Stanford, I remained in town, opting to go to our local, but nationally highly-acclaimed University of California school.

"I don't see why you can't just commute," Mother poked her head through my bedroom door. "You're welcome to stay, and you can save on rent that way."

"Mom," I said. "We've been over this how many times?" I packed the rest of my books away in boxes, which seemed to be way more than the boxes I had for my clothes, and began labeling them and categorizing them.

"Golly, Sam, the way you go about marking up those boxes…you remind me of an accountant rather than some young woman about to go off on her adventure after graduating from high school…"

"Well, if I don't mark these boxes it'll never get done, and besides, I don't want to have to dig through each one to find something I need just because I didn't label them right." I turned around, "And graduation isn't official here until next week. Then you can have all this weepy mother-daughter send off. Not right now…" I smiled. Mom have always been the younger one of us, and from looking at both of us, you'd think she was only a few years older, having had me when she was only twenty.

"I'm going to miss you moving away, Baby," Mom said.

"You have Nydia," I said, referring to my precociously cute little seven year-old sister. "And you have your friends…the ladies' group, and…"

Mom's face went from cheery to weepy in a matter of seconds. If I hadn't known better, I would have thought Mom was drunk, but she didn't smell like alcohol.

"What's the matter?" I said, dropping my marker and going over to Mom. "Did I say something?"

"Oh, Sam," Mom cried. "I really screwed up. I thought going to AA was enough. I thought that's all I needed to show that I was responsible, that I was a good parent, but your father…he was able to get the judge to grant him custody of Nydia. As soon as the divorce is final, Nydia will be going with him."

It was my turn to get weepy now. If it's one thing that can do that despite all my resolve and will to keep a "stiff upper lip" as the British called it, it was Nydia. I protected her like she was my own daughter. I would protect her with my life. "Mom, don't cry," I said, crying myself. "The judge can't separate you from Nydia. Nydia needs her mother, and you're not a bad mother, Mom." I swallowed. Did I mean that?

For several years I've resented my mother for being flaky, flighty, and I guess downright fun instead of strict and forbidding like the other mother from church I've grown used to. Yes, she was drunk sometimes, and yes, she had a drinking problem, but when it came to Nydia and me, she was always there. Perhaps not always functioning…oh, what was I trying to say? She did, however, raised me to be the fully-grown young woman I turned out to be, without me having to be in rehab or in jail…

"Do you really mean that?" Mom echoed my own thoughts and doubts.

"Yes," I nodded. "Mom, you're not perfect, but you're alright."

Mom wiped her tears with her sleeve and opened her arms. "Aww, come here, Baby!" She hugged me and kissed me on my cheek. "You always know what to say, you're so smart, Sam. How did I get so lucky to be your mother?"

"Now don't make me cry, Mom…Collins will be here any minute, and I don't want to have to wash my face from smeared mascara now…"

"You don't wear mascara," Mom said. "Your long lashes are naturally that long, thick, and curly. Come to think of it, you don't wear much makeup at all." She played with my hair, already getting into her favorite Mommy mode, dressing her daughters up, like they were her dolls or something. Even at my age…

"Where is Collins taking you?" Mom asked, coyly. She went to my closet to try to pull out something of mine that she can dress me up in, but opened it to reveal all the clothes were gone, packed away in boxes the night before, right after I returned home from my dinner with Gail and Collins, too wired from everything, from seeing Collins, from getting downright sexy with Collins, and from finding out about Gail, that I couldn't sleep.

"To check out apartments," I said. "He's helping me move, himself."

"Isn't he a billionaire?" Mom asked. "Why doesn't he just hire someone…"

"Mom, that's not the point," I said. "Just because he's got money, and lots of it, doesn't mean he doesn't want to experience it himself."

"But…he doesn't have to," Mom said. "He can avoid all that back breaking work, and…"

Right when she was about to go into her lecture on the best use of time and money, the doorbell rang. At the same time, my phone buzzed, and I saw a text from Collins fly across.

CollinsM: I'm out in front. You decent or do I have the pleasure of seeing and tasting your sweet skin so early in the morning again

"Collins' here!" I said, straightening my white lace soft shift dress, and slipping on my red mule sandals. I ran to the door, and practically jumped onto him when I opened it and saw him looking even more sexier than he did last night.

"Sam," he bent down to kiss me plunging his tongue in to taste mine while he moved his hand over the back of my dress. "It's only been a few hours, but I've already missed you. I. Want. You," he said, pressing up against me.

"Um, company still..." I gasped, pulling back. "Come in."

Collins smiled and walked confidently into the house in long strides, his legs clad in jeans that hung off his hips just so to reveal his tanned smooth stomach and V underneath. Even dressed down in jeans and a v-neck grey shirt and his hair fresh out of the showers messy, he looked delectable. If he had asked, I would have a hard time refusing to move in with him. Being so close to him, feeling his body heat so close to me, smelling his masculine spicy and musk scent, instantly caused my body to ache for his touch. As much as I wanted to constantly be in close proximity to Collins and his hot lickable body, I knew both of us could lose control and end up triggering some part of us that we haven't dealt with yet, which would be worse. "So, I'm taking it upon myself to show you a few places I checked out for you."

Collins looked around my cottage-style Newport Beach home, and leaned in. "Who's here that I have to impress about taking you out?"

As if she was in the other room just now, my mother came padding out of the kitchen, with a tray of lemonade and cookies. "Collins McGregor, so nice of you to visit," she said.

"Mrs. Sullivan," Collins said. "You look lovelier each time I see you."

Mother blushed. Collins reached out a hand and said, "Here, let me get that for you. Lemonade, my favorite. And cookies!"

"My my," Mom said, "You sure are a charmer…and hot to boot!"

Now I was the one to blush. But Collins just laughed it off. He reached for one of the cookies, and when I thought he was going to take a bite, he brought the cookie up to my mouth, pressed the edge of the cookie against my lower lips and used it to open my mouth so that it was in my mouth before I knew it, and I had to take a bite with him still holding onto the cookie. In a way, it was very seductive how Collins can get me to open my mouth so easily, and with any object. When I took a bite of it, he took the cookie away and bit the cookie right in the area where I had just bitten it. When my mother wasn't looking, he stuck out his tongue and traced the rest of the area on the cookie where I've bitten while fixing his icy blue eyes on me. "Yummy."

Oh, the blood from my brain immediately rushed down to my lower body, heating me up so warmly that I had to shift in my chair. Somewhere between his biting the cookie and tonguing it, the crotch of my panties became wet. I stood up, and was about to head into my room to change panties when Collins said, "Look at the time. We have our first meeting in fifteen minutes."

Finding You Finding Me (You & Me Trilogy #2)

Mom was staring at her glass of lemonade forlornly when I nudged her. I knew what she was thinking…thinking she should have spiked her own glass of lemonade with something stronger maybe. "Oh, Collins, so nice of you to just sit and have lemonade and cookies with me. It's nice to know young men have manners like you do. It makes it easier to say yes to when he wants extra sugar, doesn't it?" she nodded at Collins.

I've never seen Collins turned red before, and he didn't, but he did almost choke on his drink.

"Mom, um, I don't even know what to say about that, but, we have to go now so I'll see you later."

"Oh, don't worry about me, Sam, you're grown now. I was practically pregnant by the time I was your age, so whatever you do, just remember, you're never too old or too young to take precautions." She looked from Collins to me and back to Collins again. Then she got up. "I have to go pick up Nydia from ballet class. You two have fun!"

"Okay, Mom," I said walking slowly away from her and putting my hands on Collins's arms to edge him towards the front door. "If you have any problems with

Nydia, call me. I can always find my way to drive her, if you can't."

"I'm fine. I'm fine," Mom said. With that, she practically pushed us out the door and slammed the door behind us.

Chapter 9

Collins didn't waste time driving me to the first apartment, which was a beautiful suite in a luxury high-rise overlooking the city that came complete with a security system and a doorman in the lobby.

"This, um, is completely not what I was expecting," I said to Collins and the leasing agent standing next to him.

"No, of course not," Collins said, taking my hand and leading me around to look out at the view, away from the eyes and ears of the agent. "It's what I'd like to see you in," he said, glancing over at me.

"It's too much. I can't afford to live here…"
Collins placed his long index finger at my lips to silence me. "Before you protest too much, Sam, hear me out. I checked out this building, its tenants, the security they have here, and how reliable the service and maintenance was

here before I even considered this visit. This is a great apartment, with that view out there, the size…one of the designers we work with can make this place look unbelievable."

"I bet the rent is unbelievable," I said. "I can't even make a dent on something like this."

Collins pulled me in for a soft sweet kiss, cupping my face with his hands. It left me breathless and a bit wobbly when I opened my eyes. "When you gave up going to Stanford, when you gave up the million dollars and chose me instead, that's when 'we' began, Sam. This isn't about you getting an apartment to move out of your parents' house and to live on your own as a college student, it's about us moving on, moving further into our relationship. It's about us finding each other, learning and discovering each other once again, and it's about us being there for each other. This, Sam, will be my apartment, too."
I was speechless for a while before I said, "but Gail…her rules about us living together…"

"Oh, I'm not going to be living here," Collins said. "Still within Gail's rules. I will, however, visit very often…like a vacation home. It's much closer to my offices here in Newport Beach anyways."

"So, there isn't another apartment to look at?" I asked.

Collins frowned. "You mean you don't like it?"

"I didn't say that," I said. "I love it. It's luxurious, glamorous, sexy, and reminds me of some kind of James Bond movie in its modern design. I love the view, too, and it seems to have a balcony that's big enough for a pool and a Jacuzzi. But it's so rich, expensive, and so…"

"Baby," Collins pulled me to him. "Remember when we first began our liaison a while back that I had some conditions? One of them was to have an appearance befitting me for social events, as a companion…"

Hazily the rules Collins had in order for us to start a relationship drafted for legal reasons, began coming back to me, including his preferences. One of them did mention about being presentable when accompanying Collins out to a social function. "So me having an apartment like this is part of that?" I asked.

Collins nodded. "Being with me will always be about this, Sam." His icy blue eyes stared into mine as he said, "It's part of who I am, Sam. I've worked too damn hard to get to this point where I can get a place like this for the woman I love. If I want to set you up in a place I like, no, actually that I love visiting and can feel like I'm coming home to, then I damn well pay for the place, too."

I stood there, torn with mixed emotions. I've never been taken cared of like this before, and I didn't know how to react to it. Collins was possessive, and in a way, that was thrilling, yet disturbing. Being so independent, though, I wasn't sure if I can handle Collins' generosity.

Just take the damn apartment already! My playful Lola side yelled. *What's so wrong about letting a hot as hell man like Collins take possession over you, dominate you, care for you, and love you?*

Because I don't want to lose myself. I countered.

You're not. It's called becoming a couple, and "us".

Finding You Finding Me (You & Me Trilogy #2)

For once, my crazy inner diva Lola made sense, and I turned to tell Collins how touch I am by him wanting this for me...wanting to set me up in a beautiful suite and taking care of me. I opened my mouth and this came out instead. "There are almost five bedrooms in this place. It's so big, I don't know how to fill it."

He took a breath and exhaled. "Look, Sam, if you really don't care for the place, that's fine. We'll find another one." He gestured for the leasing agent to walk us out.

"No, that's not it," I said. "This place is fine, it's just so much bigger than I'm used to."

"Oh, but we have privacy panels and almost soundproof walls in some rooms, that you can close down half of the house by putting up panels," the sophisticatedly-dressed, tall, and slim leasing agent said. She was a very attractive woman in her early thirties, with long dark hair swept into a smooth ponytail and emerald colored eyes. She smiled coyly at Collins. "For those special occasions when you need extra sound proofing." Her eyes looked seductively up and down Collins, which made me instantly dislike her. Didn't she see Collins was with his girl, and he was getting this place for her? "Whatever your needs," she continued on, "I will be happy to accommodate them for you." Her pretty eyes traveled down Collins' body to stop right at his crotch.

Oh hell you won't. Lola shouted.

I stepped between Collins and the leasing agent, and said, "You know what? Come to think of it, Collins, I don't like this particular place. I haven't seen the other ones yet, so let's look at those first before settling into this one."

The leasing girl's eyes narrowed, and I could swear she looked like she was growing claws out of her fingers.

"Are you sure?" Collins asked.

I took Collins aside and crossed my arms. "I thought I liked it alright, but not when that woman out there is practically trying to seduce you right in front of me. I don't like that one bit."

"Oh Baby," Collins smiled. "I've never seen you get so jealous over me. I kinda like that, but you don't have to worry about Jodi there. She doesn't mean anything by it."

"I bet she doesn't," I said under my breath. "Look, Collins, can we at least look at the other options?"

Collins looked down and then up. "Problem is, I already bought the building…Sam, I was so sure you'd want this place, once you see it completely furnished with a library room, gourmet kitchen, pool room/playroom, the tape room…" Collins' eyes began gleaming as he happily smiled wickedly at me that got my body tingling all over with desire. "If you enjoyed the tapes you've seen of mine from before, then I'm sure you would enjoy making some with me."

My heart dropped as a small panic began deep within me. As much as I knew I shouldn't, I did enjoyed watching Collins' tapes. I loved watching them enough to have watched them over and over again until I was sure I've picked up something educational.

Collins and his last condition of his agreement for us in order to start a relationship, which both fascinated but terrified me…his need or his addiction to taping the act.

I swallowed before saying, "I don't know if I can go there with you, Collins."

"You enjoyed watching it, though," he said. "So much so that you're intrigued by it, fascinated, and curious enough to want to explore it." He smiled again. "It was sensual enough to get you to want more, wasn't it? Hot enough to get you to forget any hang ups you've ever had regarding sex or making love." Collins' eyes darken with desire as he leaned in to whisper in my ears. "Bet you can't wait to see if you can do the things in those tapes, too, to me." His voice was so velvety soft, so calming and seductive, I nodded my head while he held my chin with one finger. "I've dreamed of doing it with you for so long, Sam, I get a hard-on just closing my eyes."

If Jodi wasn't there in the suite with us, I was sure we would have a repeat episode of Collins 'tongue-fucking' me up the wall. The thought of it should have scared me, should have paralyzed me as it would have in the past, but now, caused by the boldness I've gained from the tapes, it made my entire body clench in anticipation of the next time. "Yes, get the damn suite," I said hoarsely. "You've already bought the whole building, why not get the room for free."

Collins laughed, and all it did was get me even more excited.

Chapter 10

Almost a week later, right after Graduation dinner, I moved into a fully furnished suite, my clothes already unpacked and hung in the closet along with some new clothes Collins had asked a personal shopper from Neiman's to pick out. Beautiful gowns from designers like Vivienne Tam, Vera Wang, Chanel, and Oscar de la Renta, Suits and shoes from Prada, Manolo Blahnik, and Jimmy Choo.

"What is this for?" I asked when we were alone, walking into my large bedroom with the closet larger than my living room at my parents' house.

Collins kissed me and smiled. "It's your graduation present, Sammy." His arms encircled my waist, and he easily lifted me in the air, twirling me until he brought me down to kiss me again on my lips. "I'm so proud of you, Miss Valedictorian."

I smiled, relishing his warm lips on mine. "You are, are you?"

"I am," growled Collins as he edged me away from the closet and to the large bed, covered in red silk linen, "So. Very. Proud." His crotch in his suit's slacks pounded near mine, with every emphasis of the words. Even fully clothed, I can feel Collins' warmth as he bent over me while I fell back onto the soft sheets. "Now that you've graduated, let's move onto more grown up lessons, shall we?"

I giggled, happy to be finished with high school, happy to finally move out of my parents' house. "We shall," I answered.

"First rule, young lady," Collins said sternly. "You address me as "Sir.""

"Yes, Sir," I said giggling again. This was not like me at all, but I felt less restricted, I felt free.

"Turn around," Collins said.

"Why?" I asked.

He bent me over and with a swift movement, tore my skirt off. He was about to rip off my panties when he stopped and said, "I'm saving these for later. My favorite kind…the ones with the hearts."

He tugged at it until it fell down to the ground, and he picked it up, gingerly placing it in his slack's pocket. Collins exhaled and said, "You have the sexiest round ass I've ever seen. You are so damn beautiful." He placed his hands around my bottom and caressed it with his fingers. Then without warning, I felt his fingers delve deep into me, stroking me at my most sensitive spot, repeatedly until I was quivering. With his other hand, he reached up underneath my silk blouse, tore my bra apart at the front clasp, and began rubbing my erect nipples back and forth. I was writhing and moaning with pleasure, the sensations growing stronger and stronger as his nimble fingers worked me, that I cried, "Enter me or stop, but I can't take this anymore…it's so…"

"Sam Baby honey, just let go. Let yourself go, your body's asking you to. Just go with what your body wants," Collins said calmly.

"I…I…don't know how to," I said, clenching my jaw and panting in between breaths. "Oh, this is…so…" I swallowed. I was writhing in his hands, the sensations so sensitive I couldn't take it any longer.

"Let go, Sam," Collins said. "Close your eyes, savor it, and drink it all in...the pleasurable sensation. Then..." he spanked me, "Come!" he demanded.

My mind went blank when he spanked me, letting my body take full control, and when it did, my entire body quaked and quivered with an immense pleasure that had me crying out Collins' name and grabbing at the silk bed sheets with my hands.

A relaxing sensation filled me when my body slowly stopped quivering, and Collins scooped me up from the side of the bed where I was still bent over, and laid me down in the center. He had taken off his shirt, and his slacks, revealing his broad-shoulders, muscular arms, rippled abs, and long muscular legs, legs that looked so powerful. I stared at his black cotton boxers and the large bulge in front.

"Collins," I said, "I want to feel you, I want to make you feel good, too."

Kailin Gow

Collins slid down next to me and kissed my forehead. "Seeing you come like that already made me feel good, Sam. You're making so much progress, I'm so proud of you, Baby."

"But," I reached down and reached underneath the band of his boxers to touch his hot pulsing bulge and began massaging it, stroking it. It was my first time, and I didn't know what to do, but feeling it, and touching it like this felt natural.

"Don't..." Collins growled, his eyes dark with desire.

"Why?" I asked, increasing the intensity of my strokes.

"Because," Collins growled deeply, "I will have to move to the next step, and I'm not sure if you're prepared for all the mind-blowing fucking that'll come with it."

"That doesn't sound so bad," I said, getting aroused from pleasing him and anticipating the next step, as Collins called it.

"No, I'm serious," Collins said. "You are not prepared."

"Wouldn't you just stick it in?" I asked.

Collins grunted in both disgust with what I've just said, and pleasure with what my hand was doing.

"No, that's so not a romantic and hot way to put it, Sam. No, I'm talking about taking it to the next step for me. What turns me on beyond belief. There is nothing like it, and I want you to build to that with me. You won't be able to handle it right now. It's too dark."

"Collins," I said, "I'm Susan, remembered? I know all about your dark desires. I want to help. Use me as your therapy for this, Collins. Use me to get over or at least pass them." I pulled my face up close to his and kissed him passionately on his mouth, delving in with my tongue to taste him.

As wound up as he was, he immediately took possession of my mouth, turning my body over until he was on top while fully and thoroughly kissing me until I was seeing stars.

"This," Collins said, "I can do with you right now," he dipped down and pulled my shirt up, exposing my breasts which he devoured with his mouth, giving each one lavished attention. With his free hand, his fingers dipped into me again, rubbing hard and pressing hard against my sensitive spot. In seconds, I was moaning and writhing.

"Can I have another one so fast?" I asked Collins.

"Baby, you can have as many as you'd like," he grinned seductively.

"But…I've read… in all my studies," I began, thinking of what I've read in psychology.

"Stop thinking, Baby," Collins said. "Go with it or I'll spank you again."

"I can't…" I said, thinking out loud. "It's impossible."

"No it isn't," Collins said. "It's happening right now, if you'll let it. Stop thinking about it or I'll really get upset and really spank you."

"Oh my God," I clenched my jaws and grabbed fistful of the bedsheet. My body was shaking, and I threw my head back, writhing in Collins' skilled hands. "Go…go ahead and spank me. I beg you, spank me now!"

Collins slid down the bed to sit at the edge closest to me. With his strong arms, he lifted me and placed me over his lap. "Such perfection," he said, running his hands over my butt. "You are flawless, Sam, the most beautiful woman I've ever loved."

I closed my eyes, relishing his confession of love. Then he spanked me, hard.

I didn't even had time to process it, my body went into complete explosion, with a strong orgasm that lasted for a long time.

When my body subsided, Collins pulled me in close to envelope me in his arms, kissing the top of my head. "I didn't hurt you, did I? Please tell me if I ever do. I love how you look when you're coming, Sam. You look so free, wild, and happy."

I smiled up into his beautiful handsome face. "Then we should do it more often," I said.

"I'm happy to make that happen for you, Sam," he said, kissing me. "Now," he winked. "I didn't know how much you were going to respond to me spanking you, but it seems you get a lot of pleasure from it…"

My mind suddenly became alert when he hesitated. Then I fully remembered our conversations over the phone when he was Daggers and I was Susan at the Call Center. He was used to the heavy stuff. It was the way he found his release, unlike the way I just did.

"It makes me believe, Sam, that this is what I'm waiting for. You're the woman of my dreams, Sam. Not only are you so sweet and loving, so giving, beautiful inside and out, but you and I have an innate understanding and similar tastes."

"Spanking?" I asked.

"That's just an indication," Collins said. "You have a predisposition for it, like I did."

My heart began pounding. I remembered how Daggers was distraught about his dark desires and how he wanted to escape it, not embrace it. I was helping him through it, helping him become normal. But now…it seems I was being pulled into the darkness itself. Collins wouldn't agree to it, not after talking to Gail about us and hoping to get over it so there can be an 'us'.

"Collins," I said, getting up, "You said there's a next step?"

"Yes," he grinned. "My next step. Do you want to see it?"

I nodded.

He got up and pulled on a black silk bathrobe. He handed me a smaller black silk bathrobe, wrapped it around me, and tied the tie at the waist, pulling me in for a kiss. I've never seen him with a satisfied happy look on his face.

"If you look so happy every time I orgasm like that," I said, "then by all means, we should do it again."

"That's what I have in mind," Collins said, kissing me again. His arm snaked around my waist, and he pulled me with him to walk out of the bedroom and down the hall.

"Where are we going?" I asked.

"Well…I'm hungry for one, so we'll stop by the kitchen, your new kitchen for a snack, and then we'll head over to the Production Room."

The kitchen was right around the corner, and when Collins opened the refrigerator, it was fully stocked, even with containers of full meals that needed to be heated. "Remind me to give Vincent a raise," he said.

He pulled out two containers, popped it into the microwave, and when it was done, arranged the curry chicken and rice with asparagus meal on two elegant china plates. We ate in front of the large flat screen television in the living room, with Collins feeding me with big forkfuls of food. "Eat. You need your strength."

"I do, do I?" I asked. "Am I going to be running some kind of marathon anytime soon?"

"Something like that," Collins said. "I need you to keep up your strength and stamina in the next few days when we do this."

"What? The marathon?"

"No," Collins said, almost frustrated, but still in a happy mood. "My next step."

Again, my heart skipped a beat when hearing about the next step.

When we were done, Collins took the dishes away, rinsed them and placed them into the dishwasher. I was going to help clean up, but he said, "Barbara, your housekeeper will be here tomorrow to clean up."

Raising an eyebrow, I silently asked, when did I get a housekeeper?

"It's part of the deal, Sam," Collins said, noticing my raised eyebrows. Can I get nothing pass this Greek god look-alike? "You need a housekeeper. I want you to focus on your studies and work…it's the least I can do for you when you gave up going to Stanford for me." He kissed me lightly on my forehead. "You are one incredible woman, you know."

He then led me down the hallway, holding my hand in his. We reached a door at the end of the hallway that blended into the wall so it was camouflaged, as though it was a built-in door. He slipped a key into a small inconspicuous hole on the side, and slid the door open. From the side, he lifted the light panels, and the room slowly came into view.

The tapes had not prepared me for this.

All the calls between me and Daggers had not prepared me for this.

I had walked into a movie set straight out of some horror film, complete with cameras set up at every corner.

Chapter 9

How I was able to make it into Sawyer House the next day after I fainted, and Collins had to carry me back to my room, was beyond me.

When I came to, Collins was by my side, handing me some water, looking worried and disheveled. It was obvious he didn't sleep at all last night.

I took the water from him, and took a sip. The glass shook, and I realized my hands were trembling. Collins noticed too, and took the glass of water away from me, setting it on the nightstand.

"How are you feeling?" Collins asked.

"A little shaken, but I'm fine," I said.

He traced his index finger over my cheeks and scooted in next to me, resting his cheeks against mine. It felt warm, cozy, and intimate. "I was really worried, Sam," he said. "Not just that you fainted, but that you may break down. I knew it was too soon. I was too eager, too excited. I know it takes getting used to, especially for someone so innocent and fresh like you. But the last couple of weeks, you've surprised me with how quick you were adapting, how you were making progress, I thought you could make some huge leaps. I never thought…"

He trailed off, looking down.

"That I would faint," I said.

"That and the look you had before you fainted…it was as though you thought I was a monster, that I was going to hurt you."

"Collins, I knew you were into things, but I just wasn't prepared for it. I thought it was like what was in the videos, but it's not even that."

"You're scared about it, aren't you?" Collins said.

"I'm not exactly on my toes waiting to try it out right now honestly," I said. "But that doesn't mean I'm completely against the idea."

"Look," Collins said. "I would never hurt you. I would cut off my right hand before I would hurt you. And if you have such a strong disdain for what's in the

Production Room, then we can hold off on that. We'll find other ways to amuse each other. I just don't want you looking at me like that…" his voice broke, and I knew he was hurt by the way I reacted.

"I'm so sorry, Collins," I said. "Seeing the room and associating that with sex, it does scare me."

"Maybe if we slowly ease into it," Collins said. "We can try that at first, and we don't even have to be in that room…I love you, Sam, so very much. I want to be able to make love to you…I want to be your first time and your only. I want so much for us. I just don't want us to end here because we can't get over this issue."

"I know, Collins," I said. "I love you so much, too." I pulled his face close to mine and kissed him deeply, trying to show him I still loved him so much, although I knew it would be a challenge overcoming his darker sexual desires with my traumatic sexual past.

*****

It felt strange going to Sawyer House and acting like I'm the same person that I was the last time I was here, before Collins had returned from Europe and picked me up for dinner, which turned out to be a dinner plus meeting with Collins' long-time therapist, Gail, who happened to be my mentor and boss at Sawyer House.

I thought it would be awkward seeing her there in her office when I came in, but all she did was smile and waved, eating a dish of Derek's famous homemade chocolate chip cookies in front of her.

I waved back, smiling, hiding my concerned about Collins and my inability to fulfill his dark sexual needs. I didn't want to let her know after having had an incredible double orgasm with Collins. Collins could fulfill my needs fine, but I couldn't even reciprocate. What kind of a lover and girlfriend would I be if I couldn't? Would Collins seek out someone else who could fulfill those things for him?

I was wracked with insecurity sitting in my cubicle when I felt a hand on my shoulder.

"Hi, Stranger," Derek said, smiling sadly. "It's been a whole week and a half since you were here. I hope that encounter with that prankster wasn't the reason why you stayed away for so long."

"Nah," I shook my head. "That couldn't scare me from coming here and helping people deal with their problems. I'm very dedicated," I said brightly.

Derek sat down in the chair opposite of me, his usual spot when he used to train me at my desk. "Glad to hear," he said. "I thought maybe because Collins McGregor had returned, and you were graduating…moving onto Stanford…"

"Didn't you hear, Derek. I thought you knew already. I thought I told you…but I'm not going to Stanford. I'm staying here. Enrolling into the same major as you at UC Irvine."

Derek went from surprise to instant elation. "You're here to stay?" he asked.

"I'm not going to go to Stanford in the Fall, and I'm going to be going to UC Irvine, so, yes, I'm here to stay."

Derek jumped from his seat to grab me and pull me out of mine. His arm encircled my waist, lifting me high in the air. His handsome chiseled face leaned in close until he was whispering into my ears. "You don't know how happy that made me."

Finding You Finding Me (You & Me Trilogy #2)

Before I can stop him, before I can pull back, his lips were on mine, kissing me hungrily and passionately.

"Derek," I pushed him away. "Stop. I can't."

"Why?" Derek asked. "You're not going to Stanford anymore so I assume, you didn't take Collins McGregor's scholarship money, which means you didn't want anything to do with him when he left you and went to Europe. You're not seeing anyone right now, and as far as that body chemistry between us, that camaraderie between us; it's ripe for picking right now, Sam. You've known how I've felt about you, and we've been close since Collins left. He's back, and it isn't like you're suddenly spending all your time with him…"

He stopped mid-sentence when the truth dawned on him. "But you are…that's why you've missed so many days here since he's gotten back." His face went from elation to crestfallen. He bunched his fists and looked like he wanted to punch the wall. "Why him?" he asked. "I've been here all this time with you…why him? I know he's got something kinky going on with him. One of the models whom he went to a charity ball with came out and said

Collins McGregor was into rough play, and other things. I can't see you getting yourself into that, Sam. Not especially since you recoil from any intimate touch. Please don't tell me you're with Collins like that. You'll only end up hurt and worse off than before. Collins' not good for you, and…"

Derek stopped pacing and talking, his body still tense with anger and hurt from my rejection. He looked over to a spot behind me, and I turned around.

Gail was walking towards us looking very serious. "Hi Derek," she said without a smile. "Aren't you supposed to be training one of the new counselors?"

"Not today," Derek said. "Thomas called in sick."

"Oh, well…I need to talk to Sam right now. Maybe you can take over her shift for her. It may be for a while."

Derek nodded. "Sure."

"Sam…come with me," Gail led me to her office, and shut the door.

I sat down in one of the chairs in front of her desk, a plain office chair that you see everywhere…a far cry from the luxurious office Collins set her up in when he visits her for his sessions. "What is it?" I asked, worried by the look on her face.

"I just got off the phone with Collins," Gail began, "who seemed very upset. He didn't sound like himself. He sounded like his alter ego, the voice he uses when he's regressed, the younger Collins, a part of Collins when he was younger, more vulnerable."

"Daggers," I said.

Gail did a double take. "Daggers? That's the name he used when he talked to you here, right?"

"Yes, it is. I couldn't tell it was Collins at all because Daggers seemed so vulnerable, so different from Collins, who's you know…very confident. Daggers is his alter ego?"

"When he regresses and retreats into one of the more traumatic times in his life, he's Daggers. Daggers is Collins' fourteen year old self when he began being sexually abused. Practically sold into prostitution by his mother, and became a kind a sex slave to some powerful woman he still has nightmares about. Collins never got to the point during our sessions to actually name the woman."

My heart broke just hearing about Collins' childhood. "How could his mother be so cruel?"

"Drugs," Gail said. "She was high on it, and prostituted her son to feed her habit."

"Collins said his mother died when he was really young, but you mentioned how she sold him for drugs? Then he was only a child?"

"She overdosed when he was fifteen, but that one year of prostituting him like that, scarred him for life. Before then, she abused him, beat him, and took out all her frustrations on him. Poor Collins," Gail shook her head. "In his mind, he's blocked out all those years, and believed she died when he was very young."

"He must harbor so many feelings for her, I can imagine," I said. My poor poor sweet Collins. I could imagine how this beautiful blonde angelic little boy had to grow up watching his mother get wasted, beat him, and then having too support her and him by prostituting himself as a young teen. He associated love with being beaten, and then being prostituted out. No wonder why he sought out love in any way he could find it, even if it was from lovers who wanted to beat him or get beaten by him. I shuddered, thinking about the Production Room.

As though Gail knew where my thoughts were, she asked. "Did you two finally…?"

I blushed. It was almost like my mother asking that question, but with my mother, with all her flaws, it was easier to say the truth. "He brought me to the point of release twice," I said.

"You have improved," Gail said, looking impressed. "You should be proud with how you're able to get so far with being intimate with someone when before, it brought nothing by terrorizing fear."

I had to smile about that. "That's because Collins is very very good in bed," I said. "When I'm with him, it's like nothing else matters. We're in a world all by ourselves. I've never felt this way before. I've never felt this way about anyone." I bit my lips, not wanting to get emotional in Gail's office. "I wished I trusted him earlier so we could have gotten past all of this faster, but I can't worry about that now. How's Collins? Why did he call you?" I asked.

"Like I said, he's terrified you're going to leave him. He's so worried you'll be so scared of him to the point of leaving him forever."

I threw down my arms in frustration. "I would never do that because…"

"You need to talk to him," Gail said. "But first, I'm headed out to see him. He wanted to meet me for an emergency session at my Newport Beach office alone. Just him, which I think is a good idea since having you there when he's vulnerable like that will only make him retreat further. But afterwards when I can get him out of his Daggers stage, you should talk to him and reassure him of your love and acceptance. That's what he's craving, Sam. Love and acceptance from the woman he loves." Gail took a deep breath and let it out slowly. "I've been his therapist for a few years, ever since he found me when I had my practice. He was already pretty successful, and I knew who he was. But he's had such a tough childhood and life up to now. All the women he's ever known and loved in his life have failed him, Sam. I know it's a lot to ask, and I'm setting aside my professional hat and wearing my personal one…could you give him a chance? Not only does he have an intense connection to you, but an emotional one. Somehow something about you make him want to reach out to you, to become a better man."

"I'll try," I said. "I can't give up on Collins. I admit to being scared of going into that dark corner with him, Gail...I mean I don't know anything about sex or the kind of stuff he's into...but I love him and I..."

Gail got up, came around her desk, and put her two hands on my shoulders. "I know, and that's why I believe you can pull him out of it. I've never met a young woman with inner strength and resilience like you. You fall down, but you get back up. You didn't choose the easy road, going to Stanford and moving away, for a reason. You chose to stay. There's something there to be said." She gave me a knowing smile.

Coming from Gail, who have seen so much, met so many people, and what I aspired to be as a counselor one day, that meant a lot. I was speechless. I could only nod.

Gail gathered her purse and coat, heading out the door before I can catch up. "I should probably be with him for an hour to two. Afterwards, I think you should go home and talk to him, and take good care of him."

"I will," I said, following her down the hall.

When she was out of the building, I walked back to my desk. Derek wasn't there, but the green light signaling a caller was on the line was blinking. I sat down and placed my headphones on before pressing the button to "talk".

"Hi, this is Sawyer House. I'm Susan. What do you want to talk about today?"

"Uh, Hi Susan," came a young man's voice. "I'm Joe. I'm calling because I want to know what I should do."

"About what?" I asked.

"I know about something some guys at a frat party did to a girl in one of my dorms."

"What happened?" I asked. "Maybe if you tell me what happened, I can help you make a decision better."

"Well, there was this frat party, and almost everyone was drunk. Ella, the girl in my dorms, was so drunk she was passed out on the couch. One boy began fondling her, and she didn't wake up. Another undressed her, and then it got so bad…" Joe stopped talking.

"Are you still there?" I asked.

"I'm here," she said. "It got so bad, they were raping her."

"Did anyone try to stop them?" I asked.

"Most of the girls at the party were so disgusted they left the room, and the guys were egging each other on to see who could rape her next."

"You were there to see all that?"

"I'm in the same fraternity, I couldn't leave or I'd be kicked out."

"You know it's wrong, Joe. What they did is not only wrong, but illegal, and a crime."

"I know, but if I tell, the guys will find out, and they would kick me out or worst, set me up so that my future's ruined."

"Do you have proof of what happened?" I asked.

"No, I don't," said Joe. "That's why I haven't reported it yet. The girl, Ella, probably doesn't even know it since she was knocked out. If I bring it out into the open, she'll find out, and really be embarrassed, if not, horrified with what happened to her."

I sighed, getting exasperated. This was a tough one, and I wanted to tell him to risk reporting it, but without evidence, it could make the victim look even worse. Like she was a slut, instead of the victim.

"Joe, are you friends with Ella?"

"I talk to her sometimes since she's in the same dorm."

"You should talk to her and let her know," I said. "She has a right to know what happened to her, especially when she was knocked out drunk and didn't know. That's the first step. I know that's going to be tough, but you have to in order for her to deal with it and not find out later."

"If you were in that situation, is that what you'd do," Joe asked.

I felt uncomfortable then, remembering back to the Billy Incident when I was thirteen.

"I was in that kind of situation," I said. "Only it was one guy, who had bullied me relentlessly until I agreed to let him touch me."

"Sorry to hear that, Susan," Joe said.

"Trust me, Joe," I said. "If that happened to me, I'd want to know it."

"Then I'll do it," Joe said. "My conscience will bug me until I do."

"Good luck with it," I said, before switching off the "talk" button.

The green light shot back on again, and I answered, thinking it was my last caller. "Forget something?" I asked, switching back into my Susan mode.

"Um, is this Sawyer House?" a new male voice asked. There was something familiar with it.

"Yes, it is," I said. "This is Susan. How may I help you?"

"Susan, eh?" the young man said. "So this is Susan. Slutty Susan. Been sleeping around a lot lately, Slut?"

"How dare you!" I said, anger flaring out of me. "I'm hanging up on you so don't plan on ever calling back." I lifted my finger to turn off the "talk" button, but stopped with the next thing the caller said.

"How does it feel to be fucked by that billionaire playboy Collins McGregor? Bet you loved it, bet you love being slapped and spanked…"

I almost choked. Who was this?

"Think you're all grown up now, Susan? Think just because some rich pretty boy wants to fuck you, you're some clean piece of ass now?"

"Stop," I said. "Whoever you are…you're not scaring me."

"But I am," the caller went on. "I'm scaring you shitless."

"You don't even know me," I said.

"Oh, you know me, and I know you very well…inch by inch. Undressed you once, and you loved it."

"Who are you?" I repeated again, trying not to let him get to me.

"You and your daddy were such pillars of society. My folks listened to him every week, how he counseled them on their marriage, how to raise me so I'm not the white trash drug-popping addicts they were. It didn't work so I couldn't wait to see how broken your family can get. First I ruin your Pastor's kid princess image. Dirty up your prettiness. Then I ruin him. Your high and mighty father. Make him regret ever thinking I'm just poor white trash, not good enough for his daughter."

My mouth dropped open. "Billy?"

Finding You Finding Me (You & Me Trilogy #2)

There was an ugly chuckle at the end of the phone. "Thought I couldn't find you, after all these years. I'm a man now, a much bigger guy than I used to be. Your daddy can't push me around now, can't send me to juvenile detention, like he did."

"I didn't know…" I said, I couldn't have known. My mind shut down the entire Billy Incident a while back. It was as though it existed only to be my nightmares.

"Ruined my parents when I went; their marriage fell apart. I got sent to juvenile detention only to be shipped off to somewhere far away. Another state. I blame you and your father."

"You leave him alone," I said, trying to sound brave.

"I know where he is at his new church. I know where your sister is. I know all about you, been watching you, Samantha, for a while now. Maybe your rich boyfriend will try to protect you. Maybe not. I'd like to see him try, though. I'd like to see what kind of guy you'd finally be willing to give it up to really looked like."

Kailin Gow

My heart sank, and my mouth filled with bile, making me want to gag, remembering the filthy details of when Billy tried to force me to have sex with him, tried to make me go down on him. If not, he'll beat the crap out of me. I shudder in terrified horror as the memory became clearer. I was suddenly out-of-breath, my palms sweaty and hands shaking so much, I dropped the phone.

"Hello? Hello, Slut? Guess you're really scared." He laughed. "Now that I found you, I intend on making good with raping you. I'm not through with you yet."

That's when I slumped to the ground, shaking and paralyzed. I was strong, but years of torment, of physical and emotional threats when I was the most vulnerable; left me walking with an open wound.

Billy's out of jail. He's out to get me. This time, he wants revenge.

Chapter 12

"Sam! Are you alright? What happened?" Derek was crouching near me, holding me in his arms while I buried my face into his chest.

"He's found me. He's been stalking me all this time…"

"Who? Who's been stalking you?" Derek asked. "God Sam, you're so pale and you're shaking like a leaf."
"Billy," I said.

"That kid who was here to prank on us?" Derek asked. "He's been bothering you all this time?"

"Not him," I protested. "Another Billy…" a sudden wave of nausea came over me as the memory of him holding me down on the table, naked and trying to scream but muffled by his hand over my mouth, washed over me. I gagged, and Derek held me up.

"I don't...I don't want to talk about it, Derek," I said taking a deep breath to calm me down.

I can do this. I can get past my fear of the bully who terrorized me and tried to rape me that day at church.

I shuddered again, as though my body wanted to get rid of the toxic memory of that and of his threat over the phone. I have to or he will go after someone I cared about.

"Sam," Derek said, "Whatever it is, you can tell me. It's what I'm trained to do. I'm a professional..."

I looked into his kind puppy dog eyes and tried to tell him, but the shame of it, made me clamp my mouth shut. I shook my head and looked down.

Derek's hand cupped my cheeks then and he leaned in. I thought he was going to kiss me, but all he did was whisper into my ears. "It's okay, Sam. You're okay."

I want to believe him, but I can't. I shook my head. "No," I muttered. "It's not okay." Memories of Billy at school, following my every move, began surfacing like a tidal wave. Memories of Billy cornering me right when he can catch me alone, crept into my mind. His threats, his unwanted touching, his attempts at kissing me with his sloppy wet kisses. Everything about him disgusted me. My mind had locked into a trance as the memories of small details I've blocked out crept back in. How Billy smelled like sausages, how his face and hair was always oily and dirty, how he pushed other kids around and stole things from the smaller ones. Even at twelve years old when I first met him in school, he was big, big enough to hurt an innocent kid in class so badly that he had to be sent to the emergency room. Big enough to hurt his mother and father, and once a teacher when they once tried to intervene as he was beating the crap out of a boy in school.

"Sam," he jeered into my face, his breath smelling so foul I had to turn away to avoid breathing it in. "You tell anyone this, I swear I would slit your pretty throat." He then pushed me into the girl's bathroom, and fondled me while I protested. "I want to take you in your daddy's church," he said after the fifth time he groped me while I cried silently. "Next Sunday. You meet me in the All-Purpose Room after service. If you don't show up, I know where to find your little sister. And if you tell anyone, I'll cut off your tongue."

"Sam, Sam!" Derek was shaking me. "Answer me. Why are you shivering like that, why can't you say anything…it's like you're in a trance." He pulled me up and lifted me, carrying me in his arms down the hall to Gail's office.

I was conscious of what he was doing, but mentally paralyzed in fear as my mouth stayed clamped tight, afraid of Billy's threats.

"Gail's not here," Derek said. "I don't know what to do to get you out of this. Sam…please talk to me. I'm here to help. All I want is to help you."

Gail? Did he say Gail? I know a Gail, and she told me something important today. Something about someone I care about…how she needed me to help him.

Who? What did he need me to do?

"Sam," Derek said. "How can I help? What do you need me to do right now?" He ran his fingers through his wavy brown hair, and shoved it into his pants pockets. "I'm going to call Collins. Maybe he knows what's going on."

Collins? Collins McGregor…who made me feel things I've never felt before, sensations so wonderful yet powerful, my body began reliving the pleasure of it, turning warmer and warmer. "Collins!" I said suddenly.

"He's not picking up." Derek said, his back turned to me. Then he turned around, his face surprised, but ecstatic. "You're talking. Sam, you're saying something!" He pulled me to him and hugged me tight. "I thought you were out. I've never seen it before. You were completely somewhere else…"

Being so close to him, feeling his arms around me in a kind loving way, made me feel secure, and I nestled closer to him. "I'm sorry to scare you like that. I…just…all these strong memories. So painful, it's crippling. It came all at once." I shook my head not wanting to remember any of it. I focused instead on the one memory that kept me from going there in my mind, with my body. Collins, whose presence was so strong and powerful to me that I felt my lower stomach clenching in memory of the last time I felt my entire body go. The pleasure he brought to me to get me there…

"I have to go," I said to Derek, my face almost flushed. I didn't want to let Derek see me this way either or he might think it's because of him.

Too late. My body was against his, after all, and he was holding me tightly against his chest while my heart began pounding faster against mine. "Sam," Derek said, his voice hoarse and husky. "If there is anything you want to talk to me about, I'm here. You know that, don't you?" He took my hands in his and began rubbing them with his thumbs, sensual slow circles that added to my aroused state. "I care so much for you, and it hurts me to see you like that." He raised my face with his fingers so he can look me in the eye. "Sam, I mean this, if you're in any trouble, call me." His eyes dropped from mine to look briefly at my lips, where his right thumb had begun to massage. "I want you to be happy, Sam, I really do, but you have to trust me. Let go of whatever is hurting you, whoever is hurting you, and allow new happier experiences to take its place."

I stared at him while he spoke, his thumb making my lower lips swollen and aching to be kissed.

Finding You Finding Me (You & Me Trilogy #2)

Derek was talking about creating happier new experiences...well, that was what I had wanted with Collins. Collins! "Derek," I whispered.

He leaned in, thinking I wanted him closer. He closed his eyes as his lips lightly brushed mine, but I turned away. A couple of days ago, I might have kissed back, still unsure of my feelings for him and my feelings for Collins, but now, after everything with Collins, I knew I had to remain friends with Derek. I can't cross the lines.

Derek's eyes hinted at the disappointment and hurt he felt when I turned my face from his kiss, but I had to let him know. "Derek, thank you so much for watching out for me and being here right now. I better go, though."

"Sam," Derek said, "Are you going to be fine with driving or do you want me to drive you home?"

"I don't live too far from here now," I said. "I have an apartment."

Derek's eyes widened. "Sweet. Now I know where to crash with you when we're studying late into the night for a final."

"I'd like that," I said smiling, thinking of how great it would be to be in the same classes as Derek, studying Psychology. For the first time since turning down Stanford and staying, I was happy to go to college at UC Irvine.

I leaned in and hugged Derek tightly. "You've just made everything a whole lot better, Derek. Thanks." I left and walked out towards the door. "I'll see you in a few days."

"I'll take you on a tour around campus and we'll shop for textbooks together."

I smiled. That sounded so good, so safe, and so normal right now. As I glanced back at Derek, I could see how he was smiling sadly at me. My dear dear friend Derek, whose arms felt so good and secure around me…I wish I can turn that sadness away, but that would mean I've abandoned Collins, which I couldn't imagine ever doing.

Chapter 13

I drove as fast as I could to my apartment, racing up the elevators and to the front door. When I opened the door, I knew something was different. The lovey dovey atmosphere it had was gone, replaced with a sense of dread and despair.

"Collins!" I called out, running through the rooms. "I'm here, Collins…where are you? Are you here?"

I ran through the living room, the library, the kitchen, and into my room. I couldn't find him there. Was he even here?

I checked my last messages from Collins, sent an hour ago, right before I received Billy's call.

CollinsM: I'm at your place. Come home soon. I miss you. I need you. Love you so much my heart is empty without your love.

Did I waited too long to get here? Did he waited too long to see me and finally left? Why did I sense he'd be here, waiting for me? My head started hurting, and my throat was dry. I felt so thirsty all of a sudden. Drained.

I walked over to the kitchen to get a glass of water when I noticed the leather tray on the kitchen counter. Collins usually puts his car keys in that tray. Why didn't I check before? Sitting in that tray were his set of keys. But where was Collins?

My heart started pounding, thinking the worse. What if something happened? Billy…he said he'll find me. He knew about Collins, too. What if Billy did something to Collins?

I called Collins' phone and it went directly to his voice mail. "Collins," I said, "Where are you? Call me!"

There was a faint beeping sound from down the hall. I walked down there with my phone, and called Collins' phone again.

Voicemail. Then that same beeping sound in the hallway…a little louder this time because I was closer.

Finding You Finding Me (You & Me Trilogy #2)

When I turned the corner to stand in front of the wall, I knew where it was coming from...the Production Room.

I unlocked the door, and saw it slid into the wall, opening it up until it was large enough for me to walk through and into the dimly-lit room done in sensual red silk and black velvet. In the middle of the room was a large medieval four-poster bed with intricately carved wooden posts. An antique. In the corner was a gilded gold cage, large enough to fit a person. There was a reclining padded wall that looked like it can be angled.

Where did that beep come from? And where was Collins?

I walked into the middle of the room, right up to the bed. It was magnificent, a piece from the Renaissance. The bed had red velvet curtains tied to the bedposts. I touched the fabric, and luxuriated over the softness like doe's hair. I peered through the curtains to look at the bed. Maybe Collins was sleeping there? I didn't know what to expect.

No one was there, except for the softest, most luxurious sheets. I wanted to lay down in it and sleep, feeling all the exhaustion of this afternoon at Sawyer House hit me. So soft, so inviting.

Go find Collins, Girl! My Susan conscience screamed at me. *You promised Gail you'll find him and talk to him.*

That was enough to jar the sleepiness out of me. "Collins?" I called, looking around.

I heard a click, and I turned around.

From where I was standing right at the foot of the bed, I could see out of the raised platform the bed was on up to the back of the room. It was as though the bed was on a stage, and there was an entire control room in back.

I was right! As soon as I spotted it, there was a door at the back. I began making my way to the back of the room, right when I heard a familiar voice. "Sam, you're here."

I turned around and see Collins standing in the doorway. Large Bose noise-cancelling headphones around his neck. He was dressed in black slacks and a black silk shirt that was opened, as though he had just thrown it on.

Finding You Finding Me (You & Me Trilogy #2)

The sight of him like that with his gloriously chiseled tanned abs on display, pushed all thoughts of worry out of my mind replacing it with my need to run up to him and jumping on him until my legs straddled his hips. He caught me and pulled me closer while I wrapped my arms around his neck and kissed him. "Thank God you're alright!" I breathed into his face.

"Why shouldn't I be?" Collins asked, caressing my cheeks with his thumb. "Why were you so worried?"

"I couldn't find you…"

"I was in the control room," Collins said.

"The control room in there?" I asked pointing to the Production Room.

"Yes, but I went through the back entrance to get into your bedroom to shower and change," Collins said. "I didn't hear you come in at all. The control room and Production Room is soundproof, and I was listening to some music to relax."

"The control room leads into my room?" Ingenious and sexy at the same time.

"How else are we to make a quick getaway to the Production Room from our bedroom?"

"Oh you had that planned out, did you?" I teased, happy to find him safe and in a good mood, not at all what I expected from my earlier conversation with Gail.

"Of course, Sam. That was the plan when I bought this building." His beautiful blue eyes burned into mine. "I wanted everything perfect for you. I want to take care of you, make sure you have everything." He inhaled a deep breath. "I don't want you to feel any anxiety or fear. I want your first time with me perfect."

"Collins…" He was so sweet and thoughtful, and I've never felt so much care and love from anyone before. "I'm sorry I couldn't do it last time. I rushed home…to find you. I was worried about you especially the way after we left off last night…"

Collins' eyes widened with surprised. "You're worried about that?"

I searched his face, looking for any signs of Daggers, but it seemed Collins spending an hour or two with Gail in therapy earlier today had him back on his feet again.

Finding You Finding Me (You & Me Trilogy #2)

"Well, we couldn't get to your Next Step, and…"

"Baby," Collins said, kissing me, "I'll wait. I'll wait for when you're ready. I don't want to pressure you. If you don't want to have anything to do with it, I won't push you. We have all the time in the world."

"But…" I slid down his body, and led him into the Production Room. "Look, Collins. I can do this. I can walk right on in and not feel nervous or scared."

"You're not even the slightest bit uncomfortable here?" Collins asked, his icy blue eyes assessing me with concern. "Last time you were here, you almost bolted out the apartment. You had me so worried that I offended you that much."

"I didn't know what this was all about," I said. "I pictured something else entirely, but it's not so bad. This is all new to me, Collins. I've never seen or experience this kind of set up before, so it took me by surprise. That's all it was, Collins. I was surprised."

Suddenly Collins' eyes gleamed with excitement as he took my hand and led me to the bed. "I want to show you everything in here, let you experience everything in here, Sam," he said excitedly like a kid who couldn't wait to show off his new toys.

"This bed, it's a replica of a bed once used by Casanova and his lover Henrietta, whom he described as the perfect woman. Out of God knows how many women Casanova had sex with, Henrietta was his best and greatest love." Collins' voice dropped as he said, "I thought of you when I had this bed commissioned while I was in Europe."

"Collins, this is magnificent," I said, admiring the craftsmanship of the carvings.

"It's ancient, but modern at the same time," Collins said. He gave me a mysterious smirk and I couldn't help smiling back at his youthful enthusiasm.

"Look at the panels built into this bed," he pointed out a hidden panel in the bed with buttons. "This one dims the light. This one brings out music, and this one tilts the bed at different angles."

My goodness, this was something I didn't expect. But it wasn't outrageous to the point I felt uncomfortable. My mind began imagining different uses for all of these buttons, and when I made eye contact with Collins, I could tell he was thinking the same thing.

Finding You Finding Me (You & Me Trilogy #2)

"Let's forget the tour and I'll just demonstrate the bed's uses instead?" Collins whispered into my ears.

"But there's still so much to see," I joked, wanting just as much to jump into bed with Collins. "Show me the Control Room and how that leads to my bedroom. I want to see how that works."

Collins pretended to acted disappointed, but the gleam in his eyes were evident, as he was eager for me to see the rest of the Production Room's design.

"Come with me, then, up these stairs to the back of the room."

We walked to the back where there was a black door hidden along the black wall. He opened it, and we walked into a modern day Control Room, like the kind you see in a studio. There were monitors, buttons, recording and taping machines, sound decks, tapes. Even a small refrigerator. He opened another door, a half door, the size of an attic door, and showed me where it led. It opened up into my bedroom's closet, where the designer gowns Collins had given me for graduation were hanging. So that's how Collins was able to get from one end of the house to another so quickly.

"Wow," I said for lack of a better word. "You've impressed me with this design, Collins. All this for this room. Why?"

"It's all for you, Baby," Collins said. "Who knows when the mood will hit, and we want access to this room quick, and Barbara is busy tidying up our bedroom?" He almost winked. "Besides, I'm in the entertainment industry, Sam. I own multiple companies in all aspects of entertainment. Don't you think I'll like to have the best of them in here, in the home I share with my girlfriend?"

I noticed the tapes that I had watched of Collins, on the table in piles. They were the ones I had personally watched, the ones he gave me the key to the deposit box for…his most private moments.

"Are you…" I asked, indicating his tapes.

"Watching them?" he asked. "Yes, and I'm digitalizing them so I can destroy these."

"Oh, for a moment there, I thought you said you were going to destroy them."

"I was, because they're of my past," Collins said. "But, I don't need to be watching that. I need to move on with my present and future."

"You're keeping them still?" I asked, thinking about what I've seen on them. If any of that ever leaked out...

Collins smiled wickedly. "Don't worry, when I made those videos, I made sure no one can see the other participant. They can only see me. I'll be the one who gets all the blame if any tapes ever get into the wrong hands."

Collins saw the worry in my face, and came up to me to cup my face in his hands. "Those women in those tapes...they're my past. I don't keep and watch those tapes for that. You're my here and now, Sam. I want to create a new feature just for us, about us."

He pressed a few buttons on the control panel, and the bed rotated to the center, the lights dimmed, and soft pulsing music played with a sultry woman's voice singing about love. I can see the monitors in the room power up, and the bed clearly in focus. Collins had trained three cameras to the bed, from different angles. One from the front, the other from the side, and one from the top, which gave the most amazing view.

Despite my original trepidation of being taped while having sex with Collins, I was fascinated. Intrigued. It wasn't any ordinary homemade movie, sex tape, whatsoever. Whatever it was, with Collins' touch and taste, it would be beautiful.

Don't you even think of doing it. My brain warned.

But my body was saying, *What are you afraid of? Why are you always living in fear?* This is Collins, the man you love. It isn't with a stranger, it's with Collins/Daggers…who you want to help. Remember, he needs you to help him get through abusive women. He needs you to prove to him he can have a satisfying relationship, especially a sexual one with a woman who can love him.

"Collins," I was overcome with emotions. He did all this for me. I rested my hands on his bare chest, while I tiptoe up to kiss his soft warm lips. As soon as our lips touched, we were on fire.

Chapter 14

Collins lifted me up and sat me down on the control room table so that my legs straddled his waist, as he deepened our kiss with his tongue. My hands ran up and down his chiseled chest, his rippling abs, and tight butt. The Casanova bed was magnificent, but I'd rather be on top of Collins than the bed anyday.

Being in this room made me bold, reckless, and brought out a different side to me.

Collins could sense it. "Do you want to try where we left off last time?"

I nodded, unable to take my hands off of Collins, pressing closer to him. "I want to get closer to you Collins. You let me in to see a tiny bit of your world when you talked to me as Daggers, and I didn't know what to expect at first, but now…I think I can do this. I'll try, as long as I don't get hurt."

Collins kissed me tenderly. "I would never hurt you, Sam. That's the furthest thing I want. All I want from this room is to be able to bring you the most pleasurable loving experience you've ever had, to love you, to satisfy you, to take away all the pain you've ever felt and just focus on me loving you the best I can."

"But what if I want to be spanked? What if I enjoy it so much that I'm asking for you to hurt me?"

"You control it," Collins said. "I'm only here to please you, Sam. That's what I desire to do."

"Why?" I asked, the idea foreign to me. The only time someone had tried to be intimate with me was when Billy tried to rape me. My body shuddered again with the thought of Billy.

Billy. Oh crap. Billy…he's still out there, and he's threatened me again after all these years.

Collins gripped my shoulders, "Hey, are you okay?" He pulled me to him and enveloped me in his large warm arms. "Sam, talk to me, are you alright? What happened?"

I pushed all thoughts of Billy out of my head and let the room, the lights, the music, and Collins' arms engulf me. No wonder why Collins built a room like this…this fortress of fuck, and all that. Pure sensation, pure getaway, pure obsession. Nothing but pleasure.

I can get lost in here. Forget all my worries.

"I'm fine," I said, gripping Collins' shirt and pulling it off. "Nothing I want to think about."

"Then don't think, just feel," Collins said, unbuttoning my pants and pulling it down with my panties. "Aren't you glad you didn't wear a dress?" he asked. "Saved a panty from being ripped off you just now."

"I didn't know you were into conservation," I said, kissing his bottom lip.

"Very much so," Collins said. "I'm into conserving your wardrobe so I have things to tear off."

"You can always get edible panties," I smirked, my hands unbuttoning his pants, and pulling down his zipper.

"Believe me, I have some of that already," he said. "When I knew you were moving out of your parents' home to live on your own, I stocked up."

"Think you'll be that lucky all the time?" I teased, pulling down his pants.

"What do you think?" he asked, his eyes smoldering as I take in his magnificent body from head to toe.

Not only was he beyond gorgeous, hot and sexy, smart, and a billionaire; he was the most confident man I've met, wearing no underwear underneath his slacks. "You weren't going to dress like that going to your office?" I asked.

Collins chuckled. "If you were going to be there, I might, but no, all this, is because I knew you'd be here." He smirked. "Do you think I'll get 'lucky' tonight?"

"We'll see..." I said, wanting Collins more than I've ever wanted. Wanting him to erase every thought of Billy from my mind, wanting his love for me to fill me so my body memorize and associate sex and intimacy as something beautiful and good, rather than something to be feared.

Collins slowly undressed me and lifted me up so he was kissing my breasts. My mind went blank, immersed in the intense pleasure he was lavishing on them. When he raised his head to focus his smoldering eyes on mine, he said, "Which bed, Sam?" I knew he meant which room. My normal bedroom where it seems we would have plain sex or the Casanova bed in the Production Room?

I looked at my bedroom…comfortable, nice, everyday. Nothing like a total immersion.

Like strong coffee, you need something to help you get over your fear of Billy. My body and mind converged in agreement.

"Casanova," I whispered, looking into Collins' surprised, but adoring eyes.

"Are you sure?" he asked. "Don't do this because you think I want it, which I do, but because you want it, Sam. What you want matters more than what I want, Baby."

I thought about my fear of trying new things. I thought about my fear of breaking rules. For so many years, Billy had kept me in fear of messing up, of having any decent romantic relationships. So many years, my father and the people whose opinions he cared so much about, have kept me in fear of doing things outside of my comfort zone, doing anything that wouldn't be acceptable for a

Pastor's upstanding daughter to do. It kept me from living fully as a person, from growing up.

"Yes," I said. "I'm sure, with you, Collins. Only you."

Collins' eyes filled with tears. He took my hands and kissed each of my fingers. "You don't know how much this means to me, Sam. You can tell me to stop at any time, and I will, Sam. You can trust me on that."

"I trust you, Collins," I said. "I love you."

Collins inhaled deeply. "I love you, too, Babycakes."

"Babycakes?" I asked, raising my eyebrows.

"Yes," Collins said. "I'll take you there one day...my favorite bakery. But for now, I'm hungry, I need my daily dose of you..." he licked his lips before he crushed me to his chest, carrying me into the Production Room and placing me on the Casanova bed. He reached behind me, and I heard a click. "We'll start with something small."

"Small?" I laughed. "At this point, Collins, anything you begin with will be a new experience for me so if it's small, it's still something fresh."

Collins lifted my hands with his, leaning into me, above my head, and handcuffed me with soft sheepskin-lined handcuffs that came down from the bedpost. With my arms handcuffed above my head, my breasts jutted out freely, right in front of Collins. His eyes grew dark, as he stared at them. "You are so fucking beautiful," he said. He closed his eyes as though he was memorizing in his mind how I looked naked and handcuffed hanging on his luxurious sexy bed.

Without a stitch of clothing on him, I could see how much he wanted me, and how much he was holding back. As much as he was admiring my body, I was admiring his. I think that was the point, with my hands above my head, I couldn't touch him, while he reached behind me and pulled out an object. An ice cube. He sucked on it at first, and with his tongue licked the tip of my nipples. The ice cold sensation of his tongue wet against my skin made me moan. "Not cold enough?" he asked, rubbing the cube on the tip of my other nipple while licking the one still in front of him. The shock of the ice against my nipple jolted through me, and I felt my lower muscles clench. Collins took the same piece of ice cube and sucked on it before bringing it up to my lips to rub it against my lower lips. I opened my mouth and began sucking hard on it, feeling it quench my thirst, and giving a little relief to the fire that was raging inside. The room felt warmer, and I was feeling my skin began to sweat as Collins lifted my legs on top of his shoulders and mercilessly devoured my burning skin below. Not being able to move my hands or arms, I was trapped as his skilled tongue and mouth licked and bit me with small and then large pressure. Collins had the most talented tongue, and I was so aroused, I want him to pull away to kiss me. I wanted to taste his tongue.

"I want…" I panted.

Collins lifted his head for a second, looking at me with sincere blue eyes, deeply aroused, but adoring. "What do you want, Baby?"

"I want you to kiss me, Collins," I said.

"Oh, but I'm not done with you yet," he said, kissing the inside of my thighs. He crawled up my body, pressing his skin against mine until his face was facing mine, nose against nose. "Kiss you?"

"Kiss me, Collins," I said.

He moved in and opened my mouth with his tongue before passionately kissing me, entwining my tongue with his. With his hand, he continued rubbing my nipples, while the other one reach into me, two fingers at a time until he found the most sensitive spot and started rubbing.

I've never felt so much sensations all at once, heightened just by having my hands above my head. "Collins," I said, "I can't hold on."

"Then let go," Collins said.

"I can't," I said.

"But you haven't even began getting any pleasure out of this. I want to touch you so badly. I want to…" My moan was so intense as Collins' hardness rubbed against my heated clit. Was he going to finally make love to me, fuck me, as I wanted so badly to be fucked by him?

Could he? Could the heat of our passion right now tip him over to having sex normally without any of his former needs?

Finding You Finding Me (You & Me Trilogy #2)

"Just a minute," Collins said. He walked over to a chest of drawers, took out a box of condoms, placed one on, and then, right when I thought he was returning, he went up to the control room. I looked up, and I saw the camera above me on the ceiling, adjusting. The robotic camera in front of the bed tilted, and the other one to the side moved.

Collins bounded down the stairs to me, ready to continue where we left off.

"I took one look at the camera overhead, the camera in front, and the camera to the side, and began laughing. If there was ever anything I was terrified of, it was being on stage unprepared. I felt so unprepared right now. This was my first time to have sex, and it's going to be captured on camera.

"What's the matter, Baby?" Collins asked. "I thought you wanted to try this?"

He was hard as a rock, and from the look of it, I wondered how I could fit him all in.

"Baby…we'll ease into it," he kissed my jaw, my neck, and then my breasts, while his fingers trailed down my stomach to once again work on my heat.

I was responsive, but still apprehensive.

"You're so wet," Collins said, appreciatively. "That's good. It'll be that much easier for you."

"Collins," I said, feeling the tension build again. "I want you to be in me with I come…"

Collins kissed me, and his eyes half-hooded in sheer bliss. "I would like that. I need this as much as you need this, our Next Step."

He positioned himself over me, and I could feel the head right against me.

"Are you sure?" Collins asked me. "There's no turning back after this. Once we do this, Baby, you're mine. And I'm yours. I won't let anyone come between us. Your body is mine, and mine is yours."

My heart was racing. Collins was serious about making love with me. It wasn't just about sex to him; it was about love and commitment. I was so wrong about him just wanting sex for the sake of it, just to have it.

Was I that committed to him? Was I ready to forsake everyone else for him?

Before I could answer, there was a beeping sound in the room. Over and over again, louder and louder.

"God, what can that be?" Collins yelled, frustrated. He gave me an apologetic look before he sauntered over to the dresser, where he picked up his phone.

"Oh, hi, Mrs. Sullivan," Collins said, his voice immediately respectful. "Yes, she's here. Hold on a second."

Collins walked over to me, handing me the phone, after releasing the handcuffs. "It's your mother."

I stared at him in amazement and mouthed in silence, "When did my mom start calling you?"

"Hello Mom?" I said. "What's up?"

"Did I catch you at a bad time?" Mom asked.

"Well...actually," I stammered, blushing. Right, she did catch me at a bad time. The time when I was going to experience my first time having mind-blowing sex with Collins McGregor wrong time.

"I had been looking for you. Why didn't you answer your phone? Never mind, I found Collins' card and called him."

"Why Mom, what's going on?"

"I don't know what to do, Sam. Your dad has demanded sole custody of Nydia when this divorce goes through. The hearing for that is scheduled at the OC Court House tomorrow. I tried getting a lawyer for this, but your dad is a Pastor. He's upstanding, and it'll be an easy case for him to win. I don't want to spend what little money I have on legal fees to defend against that, but at the same time, maybe I should. I don't want to lose Nydia."

"I'll talk to Collins about it," I said. "Maybe he knows people who would know what to do. Where is the hearing tomorrow, Mom?"

"The OC Family Court, Judge Colleen Seevers."

"I'll meet you there tomorrow, Mom. Whatever I can do, even just being there for you, I will."

"Okay, darling," Mom said. "I love you, you know that?"

"Yes, I do," I said. "I love you, too."

"See you tomorrow."

"See you, and don't worry, we'll figure something out."

She hung up, and I turned to Collins.

"Collins, my parents' divorce is almost finalized, and they're holding a hearing on who gets custody of Nydia." My voice broke thinking about my little sister, and how sad it would be for her to only live with one parent now. In fact, all of a sudden, I'm feeling an avalanche of sadness. My parents were getting a divorce after all these years. The family I knew of would be no longer.

Collins placed my black silk bathrobe over me, after slipping one on himself. "Don't worry about it, I know a couple of people at that Court. I'll talk to them."

He hugged me, enfolding me close to his chest.

"I'm sorry we didn't make love," I said.

"There's nothing to be sorry about," Collins said. "Don't apologize. It should come naturally, and if now's not the moment, then it isn't."

He kissed the top of my nose, before getting on his cell phone. "Well, looks like I'll be busy working out a few details for tomorrow's hearing," he said. "Why don't you take a hot shower, and I'll give you a massage afterwards?"

I smiled. Maybe the night wasn't completely shot.

Chapter 15

It turned out we didn't have much time to do anything afterwards. I showered and went to bed. As soon as I hit my pillow, I was out like a light, and didn't feel Collins join me in bed until much later that night. He seemed preoccupied when I woke up for a little bit, although he was sitting in bed, typing away on his laptop, while massaging my back with another hand.

When I woke up the next morning, Collins was still in the same position, but he had taken a shower and had changed. I laid on my side, admiring his just washed messy hair and beautiful profile. Still in silk pajamas, freshly washed, he looked younger and happier, although a little serious at the moment. His icy blue eyes were intensely on the screen in front of him.

I knew he would have worked in the office in the other room, but somehow he felt he should be here with me on the bed. He was right. I slept peacefully with him nearby, and woke with a happy smile on my face.

My heart warmed thinking about how caring he was throughout our lovemaking yesterday, and how he thought about everything I needed or will ever need for this apartment. I've never felt so loved and well-cared for by a man before...a man as desirable as Collins. Even in just pajamas, he was hot. And he smelled so good - masculine, warm and clean at the same time.

With a hint of cinnamon vanilla. I inhaled the delicious scent of him, and said, "Hmm, you smell so good, I can eat you!"

Collins stopped typing, and glanced over at me, his lips turning up into a wry smile. "That must be the cinnamon rolls Barbara is baking for breakfast."

"She's here already?" I asked.

"Yes, you should meet her. She'll be coming in everyday except weekends to cook and clean up."

"Cook? Collins, I can do that for myself," I said.

"Since you've moved in, you haven't," he said. "There's nothing in the cabinets except peanut butter and jelly, some bread, a box of dry ramen noodles, and a can of tuna. Vincent and I helped stock up your kitchen the first night you moved in, but after that, you haven't had anything in the refrigerator.

"Collins…"

"No Collins me," he said. "You need to start caring for yourself, especially remembering to eat. I notice you skip meals once in a while or hardly eat at all. I'm worried about that, Sam."

"Well, you don't have to," I said. "I'm fine."

"You don't even have to think about it, Barbara will do the shopping for you and plan the meals. Don't worry, she'll work with you in getting what you want."

"Sounds great," I said.

Collins grinned. "Think of it this way, Babycakes, it'll give me more of your time…and judging from how insatiable you and I are with each other, whatever extra time we can get, just to be together, is worth it."

I sat up and crawled over close to Collins and kissed him. "I love spending time with you, Collins."

"So you're not upset I hired someone to cook for you?"

"Are you kidding me?" I asked. "I'm grateful I have such a sweet and thoughtful man as my boyfriend."

With that, Collins pulled me over so I was sitting on his lap facing him while he kissed me. After pulling away, Collins said, "As much as I'd like to continue all day kissing you, it's time to get ready. Court hearing today remember?"

"Yes," I got up, went to the bathroom and got ready, emerging out of my closet in a dark blue sheath dress with matching blazer. I knew it was a bit formal for me, but according to Vincent, who once worked in court, that's how you dress in court.

*****

We arrived at the Courthouse and met with my mother, who was dressed in a suit. She was dressed appropriately as usual. Despite having a drinking problem, which she claimed she no longer had, she always knew how to dress.

"Thanks for being here," Mom said, approaching Collins and I.

"My lawyer is flying in," Collins said. "He should be here this morning." Collins looked nervously around, and said, "Any minute now."

"They moved courtrooms," Mom said, looking at the schedule. "Everyone's going to be almost late, but let's get going."

Collins took a look at the schedule, and for some reason, his face froze for a second. He shook his head, reached into his grey suit pocket, and brought out his phone. "I'll let Howard, my attorney know about the room change," he said, and walked off to the side.

"How are you feeling, Mom?" I asked, walking close to her, while Collins is walking behind us, talking on the phone.

"Oh, worried, that's all," Mom said. "I know your father would be a good parent to Nydia. He loves her and would take good care of her, but I'm her mother, and…"

I reached over to hug Mom. I know what she meant, despite Mom's problems with alcohol. Despite that, she was always there for Nydia and me. "Mom, we can't worry about the past, just the present and the future. We have to be positive about this. Maybe the judge, if she's nice and have a heart, would grant joint custody instead of sole custody."

"But I'm..." Mom started to say.

"Mom," I said. "Look at me. You have to think positive about this. You're doing everything you can to be a better person. You're going to a support group for drinking. You're trying to stop, and you have for a while now, right? That's what you said last time we talked."

"But I failed as a mother. It's on the records," she said. "I failed to protect you from almost being raped by that psycho boy back home."

Billy? Mom was referring to Billy?

"It's not your fault, Mom."

"His parents attended our church. Your father was counseling their whole family about Billy. We just never knew he was out to get you the entire time."

Finding You Finding Me (You & Me Trilogy #2)

"Mom…" my head was reeling. I didn't want to think about Billy and how long he tormented me in school…so much so that I shut down whenever a boy wanted to touch me. "Mom, let's not talk about him."

"But it's on the record, Sam. Your Dad and I put Billy in jail, in juvenile court, for attempted rape and assault. You didn't know at the time what happened to him, and we made up a story about him moving away with his family, but after what your father heard through counseling with his family, he thought it was best to put him behind bars."

My mind woke up. "What did Dad hear?"

"He didn't know who the girl Billy was talking about, but he was obsessed with a girl he knew, and he said she was a walking orgasm waiting to happen, and he wanted to teach her a lesson for leading him on and…"

"That Son of a Bitch!" I said. "That was all in his sick mind."

"Baby…Honey," Mom said. "I'm so sorry. Your father and I should've known it was you. We should have protected you from that sick kid. The way he described you, it was a completely different person. We thought he was being teased and led on by a cruel girl in school, one of the pretty popular mean girls who liked to step on boys' hearts. That wasn't you at all!"

"Mom…" I was trying so hard not to cry. "You have no idea what he put me through…"

Mom reached over and hugged me. "I'm so so sorry, Sam. I'm not worthy to be your mom, but I'm so damn proud to be."

Now I had tears in my eyes. "Mom, it's not your fault. Please don't blame yourself. But you have to kick this drinking habit. It's not good for anyone. That's not to say you can't have something in moderation, but Mom, you can't get to the point where you're drunk and…oh, I better stop. You know what you have to do, Mom. When you get up to tell the judge your side of the story, remember…you're doing everything you can to be a good responsible parent. You love Nydia, and you'll do everything to protect her and keep her safe."

"I love you, too, Sammy Baby," Mom said, tears streaming down her face.

"Oh no, we can't be crying, not now, not before the hearing," I said, taking out tissue paper from my purse and handing it to her.

We were standing in front of the double doors to the Courtroom, but I can see the ladies' room to the side. Collins was way behind us, still talking on the phone. I took Mom's arm and led her to the restroom. "Mom, we have to freshen up. No tears, no looking tired or incapacitated. We have to look our best, be positive, and upbeat. We're going to win this!"

Mom glanced over at me while applying fresh lipstick. "You know what you just sounded like?" she asked.

"What?" I asked, applying lip gloss, then brushing out Mom's hair.

"That blonde lawyer girl from that movie...*Legally Blonde*. So positive! I adore Reese Witherspoon." Mom said.

"Well, it worked in the movies...maybe it'll work right now," I said, leading Mom out of the restroom and headed back to the courtroom.

Collins was standing there with a tall gentleman with grey hair and a nice dark tailored suit.

"Howard, here they are. Mrs. Sullivan and her lovely daughter Samantha Sullivan."

Howard's charcoal grey eyes appraised us both, but landed on my mom's eyes. "I can see where the lovely daughter gets her loveliness," he said smiling charmingly at my mom. Did my mom just blushed?

Collins and I exchanged looks, and his lips turned up at the outer edge, suppressing a smile. I didn't expect Collins' lawyer to be that handsome and distinguished looking.

We both glanced back at my mom and Howard. They were busy talking about the case, but it seemed there was some serious chemistry going on between them.

OMG, I could not believe what I was seeing…

"So," I walked up to Collins, wanting to kiss him for bringing a guy like Howard here to help my mother out today, "where did you meet this riffraff off the streets?"

"Off the streets," Collins said, noting my sense of humor.

Finding You Finding Me (You & Me Trilogy #2)

"Think this guy is a tad too plain-looking for the courthouse?" I asked.

"I should've gone with a modeling agency, but at least Howard's from one of the top law firms. He's the one who's been working on getting my Tate out of jail."

I took Collins' hand, squeezing it. Collins had been working on that for a while now, and was about to have his brother released to him when he stopped all procedures. "If you don't mind me asking, how is that going?"

I didn't mention anything else about Tate, and how finding out about him and Collins' plans for him and me, nearly drove us apart a few months ago.

"Tate's out. Just like that. Seems like he's been out for a while now, when I was in Europe."

"How? How did he managed that when you've been trying for years…"

"Simple. My good-for-nothing deadbeat dad got him out. He's still his legal guardian, and with all the framework Howard had built up for the release of Tate already in his files, all my dad had to do was sign some papers, then Tate was free to go."

Collins stared blankly ahead, his mouth grim.

"Why aren't you happy about that?" I asked.

"Because…" Collins let out a deep breath. "Tate is well…complicated. I wished I got to him earlier in his life before he turned out to be the asshole that he is now. He's reckless, easily-influenced, hormonal, smart, and diabolical. Unfortunately, I see everything that I was when I was living off the streets on my own as a teen, in him. If I can turn him around…he can have a better life."

"So why the glum look?" I asked, putting my arms around his neck to kiss him softly on the lips. Why did Collins looked so distracted and tortured all of a sudden.

"I hear he's gotten into some bad circles already…thanks to my asshole father. I don't know what my father is planning, springing Tate out of jail like that. I've never heard from my father since I got out of jail, and that was a long time ago. He wanted me to join in his crime ring, but I refused. For obvious reasons. I'd rather go on living on the streets than join him. Thank goodness the man who helped me become the man that I am today came by later in my life, like it was Godsend, and helped me pick my life back up."

"You can still do that with Tate," I said.

"I wished I could, but from what Howard tells me, Tate is pretty hardened. He was much harder than I ever was. I was in jail briefly mainly for loitering because I didn't have a place to go, but Tate…he's doing hard time for robbery, assault, and carrying a conceal weapon."

"You're leaving something out," I said, my intuition kicking in.

Collins smiled. "My smart and sexy Valedictorian…I knew you were more than a pretty face."

"Well, what is it?" I asked, looking at him directly in the eyes.

"Attempted murder," he said.

My mouth flew open. This was the boy Collins was originally going to have me tutor when he got out?

"I know, Sam, I should have warned you, and I know better now that it's not fair for me to expect you to help me with such a troubled kid as him. He's dangerous, and it was a dumb idea of mine to think he can be trusted around someone like you." Collins kissed me on my lips softly and then firmly. "Once he gets a whiff of you, he'd be all over you, Baby. I'm making sure there is no way that he does."

"Collins! You overestimate me. I'm not some kind of siren or she-devil who lure men away…"

"You are to me," Collins said. "And judging from every man I've seen next to you, you have that pull…"

I playfully hit Collins in the shoulders. "Oh come on. That's because you're biased, and I love you for it." I kissed him.

He deepened the kiss with his tongue, "I love you," he growled. "I can't wait to get this over with so we can go back to what we were doing last night."

"You do, huh?" I said.

"I'm feeling pretty 'lucky' after this," Collins said.

"We'll see," I said, walking off. "Time to head in. Hope we're all pretty lucky today."

Chapter 16

It was strange seeing Dad in court sitting on a separate table from the one Mom and Howard sat on. Collins and I sat in the back.

I was wondering where Nydia was, but glad she wasn't here to see how Mom and Dad would be acting or to hear the accusations that would come up. She was still in kindergarten. She didn't need to hear anything that would be said here today.

There were a scattering of people in the room. Some people from church, including Pastor Michael, who sat in a chair on my father's side. His warm eyes met mine when he turned around to see me sitting at the back of the room. He smiled, and there was a look of longing on his face as he looked. Then he noticed Collins sitting next to me, his face grim, his eyes shooting daggers at Michael for even giving me a too friendly look. I haven't talked to Michael for a while, since Collins came back.

Michael got up and came over to the row in front of me and said, "Sam, I haven't seen you in a while."

I don't know if that was for Collins' benefit or mine, but I smiled. "I know. I haven't been to Dad's church ever since this started. It's awkward you know," I said.

"Tell me about it," Michael said. "Both of your parents are good friends of mine. I don't even want to get into the middle of it, but your father asked me to come today. So here I am."

"I know my parents want to keep everyone from church from finding out," I said.

"Unfortunately, the truth is, there will be some talk, but I'll try my hardest to divert any embarrassing gossip away," Michael said. He looked over at my Dad, sitting there, looking so composed with his lawyer. "You do know that after this, your Dad's going on vacation. I'll be running the church until he gets back."

"No, I didn't know that," I said.

"He's going to take some time off, spend it with Nydia, take her to Disneyland and all the places she wants to go. Be more of a Dad to her."

I gulped back some tears. Dad never wanted that with me. I knew why, too. Mom told me a few months ago that I was never his. No wonder why he'd always treated me with indifference.

"Sam," Michael leaned in closer so he can talk to me in private. "I could really use your help at church while your father is gone. You know the procedures, you know the music, and you can help run the youth group while I take over your father's duties. Without you, I don't think I can handle running the youth group, choir, and run the entire congregation."

"I'm starting school at UC Irvine," I said.

"You are?" Michael's obvious joy couldn't be contained. "You're not going to Stanford?"

"No," I said.

He pulled me into a hug, which made Collins stand up. "Congratulations on UC Irvine," Michael said. "I knew you'd amount to something…"

"Oh, stop," I joked.

"So would you at least think about it, especially

now that you're staying in the O.C.?" Michael asked, ignoring Collins, who was staring Michael down.

"I will," I said.

"Good," Michael said, his eyes caressing me. He walked back to his seat, and stared ahead.

"You'll think about what?" Collins asked, leaning into my ear so I can feel his warm breath tickle my skin. I shivered. Even that sent thrills down my spine.

"About helping out at church," I said.

"You'll be too busy," Collins said, taking my hand.

"School doesn't start until Fall," I said.

"You'll be too busy with me," Collins said.

"Why? I have Sawyer House, but other than that, I'll have more time to help out."

"No you won't," Collins said.

"Why?" I looked over at Collins, and he bit his lips while looking down.

"Because," he said, running his finger around my hand. "You'll be helping me with my subsidiary in Europe. You'll come with me there. We'll go on a cruise before then. I want to show you around, let you see my chalet in Switzerland, my chateau in France, my villa in Italy. I want to show you a little more of my world, Baby." He brought up my hand to kiss the knuckles, and then leaned in again to whisper. "I'm so crazy about you, Sam, I can't see straight. And I'll do anything to keep you from spending your time at your father's church, 'helping' that young pastor friend of yours who only want one thing, and you're too innocent to pick up on that."

"Michael wouldn't do that. We're just friends. But you're serious about going to Europe with me?" I asked.

"Yes, Baby, I am. I still have so much to do there. I would have stayed, but when you told me you're not going to Stanford, and I knew the reason behind it, I had to return. I'm here, Baby, all because of you. Everything I'm doing here and today, Baby, remember, is all because I love you."

"Oh Collins!" I threw my arms around him and kissed him. I didn't care how I looked in court, I just knew I loved this man.

Michael shot us a look then, and I knew what Collins was saying was true. Michael looked jealous and angry, as though he really did feel something for me. I felt bad that he did, but I never knew nor did I actively encouraged it.

After we kissed, Collins sat up straight and stared ahead. The bailiff came to the front of the court and said, "Your Honorable Judge Colleen Seevers is presiding."

Everyone stood up while an exquisitely beautiful woman in her late thirties walked in, wearing a judicial black robe. She had long straight black hair, an oval face with high cheekbones, and beautiful green eyes. I couldn't tell from the robe she was wearing, but she seemed to be trimmed and elegant, too.

I was not the only one spellbound by this beautiful woman. The entire courtroom seemed taken aback. She sat down and everyone sat. "So, we have Sullivan vs. Sullivan," she began, her booming deep voice commanded the room.

She looked at my father sitting at the table, looking calm and cool. "You're the pastor of a large congregation in Newport Beach," she said. "I know you have a reputation to keep up so we won't be mudslinging here in court today."

She looked at my mother sitting with Howard at the table across from my father's. "That goes for you." She looked at everyone in court, her bright green eyes assessing the room. When she spotted Collins sitting next to me, she stopped. Her eyes seemed to devour him for a moment while her tongue shot out to lick her lips.

"We'll leave all the he says she says and sob stories in the bedroom where it should be. I read all the files you submitted to me, counselors, and I thank you for making it well-organized and easy-to-follow." She looked at Collins again, a smile on her face.

"Mrs. Sullivan has shown remarkable progress in her support group, it seems," she flipped through pages and pages of paperwork. "I commend you for making the effort and putting your child first," she said.

"Thank you," my mother said.

"And you," Judge Seevers nodded to my father, "Your plans to spend more time with your daughter this summer is noted. It will do you and everyone some good to take time off to spend with your children. They're only this age once so make the most of it."

"Thank you, I will," my father said.

"So the court appoints Pastor Sullivan and Mrs.

Sullivan joint custody of Nydia LeeAnne Sullivan. Case rests." At that, the judge stood, gathered her files, and walked out of the courtroom. Before she left, though, she turned and glanced back at Collins with a smile that would have made me burn with jealousy had Collins not told me he loved me minutes before.

I ran down the aisle to my mother's table and gave her a big hug. "You did it, Mom!" I said. "You have joint custody of Nydia. That's so much better than before."

"Yes, it is!" Mom said, her eyes tearing up.

"Thank you, Howard," I said. "I don't know what you did since you only had less than 24 hours to do all this, but thank you anyways."

Howard smiled and looked a little sheepish. "I just filed some paperwork I got from some sources. The one to thank is Collins. He's pulled some strings, and this time, he really asked for a huge favor." Howard glanced over at where the judge just departed.

"The judge?" I asked. "They know each other?"

Howard nodded. "She was the one who got him out of jail when he was a teen."

"Oh," I said. "So she's a friend of Collins. That's

great, I'd love to meet her and get some insight into him…"

Howard laughed. "I'd suggest if you want any insight into Collins at all, you'd have to talk to him yourself. He's pretty mum and mysterious to all of us."

I turned to head back to Collins but couldn't find him anywhere in court. I walked out of the room, thinking he was outside, taking a call. I turned and walked down the hall to see if he was near the restrooms, but he wasn't.

Then I heard some voices. Collins and a female voice.

I walked closer to an area close to the courtroom where the voices were louder. They were coming from a hallway hidden behind the courtroom, but the vent where I was standing allowed me to hear part of the conversation.

"I'm with someone I care about now," Collins said. "I don't want to hurt her. She's not used to the lifestyle. She won't understand."

"But you know what I did out there, didn't you?" came the female.

"Yes, thank you," Collins said.

"So you'll meet me at the club, won't you? For old

times' sake."

"I'm through with that. I'm not into that anymore," Collins said. "I'm trying to have a normal relationship…"

"But you love what I do to you," the female said. "You've always have ever since I took you out of jail, took pity on you, and taught you what it is like to have love and pleasure."

"No, you taught me to be your sex slave, if nothing else!" Collins said.

"No you were a very willing participant, I recalled," the woman said.

"No, I was a teen, a minor under 18, and you took advantage of me and my situation," Collins said angrily.

"I showed you love. I loved you, Collins. We would have been beautiful together," she said. "You know you desire me. You never forgot me. I bet you were trying to find a girl to be my replacement with this new so-called love of yours, whom I just did you a big favor for."

"That's not true," Collins said.

"Then why are you responding to my touch right now, Collins? You're getting so hard, we can do it here in the hallway and no one would know."

Finding You Finding Me (You & Me Trilogy #2)

"Keep your hands off of me," Collins said angrily.

"You may say that, lover boy, but your body is humping me right now, and why aren't you stopping me from slipping my hand down your pants to play?" A moan. "You feel so hard and hot, I'm going to unzip your pants and…"

"No, Colleen!" Collins said. "I don't even know why I agreed to talk to you again, but I'm here because of her, not you."

"Really," she laughed. "I took a good look at her sitting in my court today. If you haven't forgotten me, I don't know what. She looks like my doppelganger. Same hair, eye color, and even body type. Really, Collins, you should pay more attention to your subconscious. It would have told you your new girlfriend is a replica of me, your original love…before you get all high and mighty with me."

I couldn't listen anymore. My heart was in my throat. I was shocked. I had so much respect for the gorgeous judge that I just admired in court. But she and Collins had been lovers?

I couldn't refute that from the conversation. And she was right. We did share the same coloring. I did look like a younger more innocent version of Colleen Seevers.

I couldn't stand it. I ran into the restroom and threw up.

Get yourself together! You have to show you know nothing.

Oh shut up! I told Susan.

I let the tears fall, and when I was done, I head back outside where my mother and Howard was waiting.

"Where's Collins?" I asked.

"He texted me with a message saying he had an emergency he had to deal with and to please take you and your mother home," Howard said.

How could I tell Mom that the reason she won was because my boyfriend had promised a favor from the judge? How can I tell Howard that?

"Fine," I said, looking at my phone. There were a few texts from Collins. One of them saying he had an emergency, and he apologized he can't take me home.

My heart dropped. Was Collins really going to go meet her?

Finding You Finding Me (You & Me Trilogy #2)

When Howard dropped me off at the entrance of my apartment building, I went straight up to my apartment, wanting nothing more than to take a shower and sleep, feeling emotionally exhausted and drained. Afterwards, I didn't know what I was going to do.

I gave up my dreams of going to Stanford partly because of him, and I almost gave up my body to him. I knew that he loved me or he wouldn't have gone through such lengths to be with me. But was I enough for him sexually and emotionally to get him to heal and turn away from his past?

Chapter 17

I didn't even make it to the showers.

The door slammed shut behind me as soon as I opened the door and walked into my apartment.

A large hand covered my face, my mouth, while I struggled to free myself. I stepped down on the masked intruder's foot, which caught him by surprised, and elbowed him as hard as I could. He let go of me long enough for me to turn around and use the palm of my hand to push up into his nose, throwing his head back.

He stumbled, and that gave me the chance to try to run out the door, but another masked assailant blocked the door. Was there another way out?

Finding You Finding Me (You & Me Trilogy #2)

I ran to the nearest door near me...my bedroom. The assailant blocking the door followed me, getting close enough to grab at my hair.

He pulled me back before my hands could reach for the door, and I fell into his chest, pushing him down. His body broke my fall, but I was trying to stand up. Wearing a dress and heels today was not the best outfit to run in. I didn't care. I had to get away.

"Don't run!" his voice shouted.

"Like hell I won't," I brought my knees to his groin as hard as I could, causing his hands to fall off me while they grip his balls. "If you touch me again, there's plenty where that comes from."

I glanced over where the other assailant was supposed to be, but didn't see him.

If I head into my bedroom now, I knew I would be trapped, and then I'll have to wait it out, but if I tried to make a run for the outside door, I could get away.

I decided to go for it, but reached into my pocket, and pressed an emergency button on my phone. I didn't know who to call, except Collins, but most likely he was still busy. I hit 9-1-1 instead, and then left a brief message with Collins. "Trouble. Here in Apt. Help!"

It would take a few seconds for me to reach that door and I'll be out, running for the building's security.

Too late, as soon as my help message sent, a hand grabbed my hair from behind, and I was pulled back into the arms of the first assailant. This time, he was prepared for a fight.

I lashed out with my elbows, both of them, but couldn't make contact as he swerved his torso to miss my blows. My heels were trying to stomp down on his feet, but he knew that move already. So I bent forward, using my butt to crash into his groin and my weight to make it hurt, and tried to slip out of his grip.

He let out a yell and moved back, but with one arm, he still held my waist. "I love this fierce side of you, Sam," he said through his mask. "It's very sexy. Oh you are making me so hot for you, I can't wait to fuck you over and over again. Me and my friend there."

My heart stopped, and I was paralyzed for a second. I knew that voice so well. It's haunted me for so long. Billy.

Finding You Finding Me (You & Me Trilogy #2)

My body reacted by wanting to recoil in fear.

Oh no, I cried inside. This is not happening. My body was shutting down.

Billy pulled me to the sofa in my living room and sat me down. He took off his ski mask, and threw it on my table. He smiled, his white teeth grinning like a toothpaste commercial. The breath in me was knocked out as I stared at him. He had grown, like I had. Instead of the awkward teen that tormented me, he was now a man who was about six foot two inches, with muscles, a gash near his blue eyes, and another near his temples, leading to his dirty blond hair. He looked like a surfer and the handsome boy next door football player, rather than the boy who molested me throughout junior high and then tried to rape me.

He sucked in a breath before sitting right next to me, putting his hand on my thigh, which I tried to push away. "You are looking really good, Sammy."

"I have nothing to say to you," I said, trying to turn away.

"Aww, Sammy, is that the way to treat an old friend?" Billy said, moving his hand up my thigh headed in the direction of what was underneath my skirt.

"You are not my friend," I spat.

"Oh but I am. We've known each other for how long? You're the first girl who was ever nice to me."

"My mistake," I said, trying to move away from him.

"Oh, don't be that way, Sammy," he said, his face moving closer to me. "You smell so good, and you're pretty now than you were when we were kids."

"So now you're nice to me?" I asked.

"I was always nice to you," Billy said.

"Touching me and fondling me against my will, forcing me to do the things you wanted me to do to you by threatening me? All that is being 'nice' to me?" I spat. "You are one sick…" I stopped.

He was looking at me with a crazed manic look in his eyes. "Ah good times," he said. "You're the best girlfriend I've ever had."

"I was never your girlfriend or anything," I said.

Finding You Finding Me (You & Me Trilogy #2)

"But you were nice to me," he said. "Friendly to me, let me hang out with you at church and at school sometimes."

"I was being friendly. That is a far cry from being your girlfriend," I said. From the crazed look in his eyes, I knew I was talking to someone who was mentally unstable, stuck in some kind of sick fantasy world which he thought I was part of. There was probably no reasoning with him, but at the moment, it was a way for me to buy time before the police would arrive or Collins.

Billy leered at me, his face filled with lust. "You are one hot babe, you know that, Sammy. Always were. What guy wouldn't want to bang you when they can?"

"You don't have permission to, Billy. It's my body, it's my will. You. Don't. Have. The Right. To Touch Me!" I yelled into his face.

Billy backed off and got up. "Wow, bitch alert." He gestured to me to his friend who still had his mask on, sitting at the kitchen counter. "Must be because she's with a rich boyfriend now so she's so high and mighty," Billy continued on.

He laughed. "This is the perfect plan. I get to have my cake and eat it too. I get to have Sammy, do what I want with her, while you get to collect the money from the boyfriend." He laughed again. "Like your kind of thinking. You're a smart one, if not just for a kid."

The assailant got up from the bar stool and walked over to me, his eyes bright blue and looking at me with interest. He licked his lips. "She looks prettier today in that dress than when I saw her at the Center."

What? I've seen him before?

He came over and raised his hand to touch my face. Softly and then reverently. He looked over at Billy and said, "We keep her as hostage only."

"What?" Billy asked, angry. "I thought you said I can do whatever I want with her."

"That's before, now I've changed my mind," the boy in the mask said.

I tried to see his eyes again. Maybe I can figure out who he is by his eyes? Blue eyes? Where have I seen them before? They were almost the same shade as Collins' light icy blue ones, but his eyes were wider, not as kind as Collins eyes, but…

- 195 -

Finding You Finding Me (You & Me Trilogy #2)

"Tate! You promised," Billy said.

Tate. The name hit me like a punch. Tate. Collins' brother who just got out of jail.

"I didn't promise that you can hurt her," he said, looking at me and licking his lips nervously.

"So what are we supposed to do with her?" Billy asked. "I know what I want to do. Been dreaming about it for years." Billy turned to me and said, "You know, Sammy, I masturbate to you when I go to sleep at night. Does that make you feel powerful? Does that make you want to slap me?"

I clench my teeth. Despite Billy's football player looks when we were in school, there was always a reason why I never felt attracted to him. He was mean, smelled badly, and would torment me. "Billy, whatever sick universe you came from, saying all that and threatening me like that will not make me want you."

Tate came over, and took my hand leading me to a seat at the kitchen counter. "Don't mind him. He's a sicko. He's dense in the head. Wouldn't know the difference between a lady and a dog."

"Tell me something I don't know, Tate," I said. His eyes ran from my eyes to my lips and back to my eyes again. He licked his lips nervously.

"Gosh, my brother is one lucky SOB," he said looking around the apartment and then fixating his eyes on mine.

"Why?" I asked.

"He's got all this," Tate said. "He doesn't have to worry about anything. He's got a girl like you."

"That's because he's worked hard for it, Tate. It wasn't always like this for him, you know. He had it bad when he was younger…about your age, I think."

"I'm not a kid, if that's what you think," Tate said.

I looked at him from head to toe. No, he wasn't. He was tall, about six foot, and muscular, built like a quarterback. Looking at his body, I would guess he was eighteen or even twenty. "No, you're not," I said. "You're a man, I can see that clearly."

This brought a smile to Tate's face. "So I keep telling everyone."

"So how old are you, Tate?" I asked.

"I'm fifteen," he said. "I'm not that much younger than you, Samantha," he said, licking his lips nervously again.

"You know how old I am?" I asked, looking at him through his mask.

"I…I know about you," Tate said. "I've seen a photo of you, and then I found you online. Then I read in one of your posts that you were working at Sawyer House." He shuffled his feet, looking down. "I called once and got a Susan. I knew Susan was you, Samantha. I heard your voice on your father's church welcome video on the website. Collins mentioned you once when he visited me in jail. I just had to meet you."

"We were going to meet," I said. I gulped remembering how Collins wanted me to befriend Tate, be his tutor, and maybe even a possible girlfriend before he realized that he loved me and wanted me for himself. Now the irony of it all. I was facing Tate, whom Collins had planned for me to meet from the start. But under completely different circumstances. "Look, Tate," I said.

"What you're planning with me and Collins, it doesn't have to be this way."

"You don't understand," Tate said. "It does. Collins closed all doors of communication on me. One day, he stopped trying to get me out of jail legally. So the only other recourse was for me to accept our dead beat father's proposal in order for him to get me out of jail."

"Tate," I reached out my hand to take his. I never felt the need to communicate more clearly than this moment. "You can get out of it. Come stay with Collins and me, and we can help you get back on your feet again." I looked at him deep in his wide blue eyes.

"You mean that?" Tate asked.

"Yes, I do," I said. "I mean it with all my heart, Tate. I want to help you."

Tate visibly inhaled, his eyes glistening with unshed tears. Thank God, he could cry I shouted inside. That meant he wasn't a psychopath like Billy. He could feel.

"Let me help you," I said, taking both of his hands into mine now. "I don't want to see you go back to jail. You have so much potential. I can see that, Tate."

"Why do you care?" Tate asked so softly.

"Because I see Collins in you, Tate. He was once where you are. He lifted himself up to the man that he is today. I can see you doing the same, Tate. You have it within you. You just need to believe you can go on the right pathway and not fall back into being in jail, wasting away your life like that."

"I can almost believe you," Tate said, closing his eyes. "I want to believe you."

"You'll have to stop this plan you have with Billy before anyone gets hurt," I said softly, not wanting Billy to hear.

"It's more complicated than that," Tate said. "Billy's out because someone sprang for him, paid for his bail, and pulled some strings, too. We both owe my dad and his partners for us getting out of jail. Now we have to do whatever they want to pay them back."

My heart fell. It was more complicated than I thought.

"Hey," Billy's obnoxious voice boom from across the room. "I'm getting hungry. So Mr. Brains, what are we going to do?"

"Do you have anything to eat?" Tate asked.

"In the refrigerator," I said, thinking Barbara stocked it already.

"I check the fridge already," Billy said. "As soon as I got here and was waiting for her to show." He came over and said, "Go make that phone call to your brother, man. It's time."

"I've changed my mind," Tate said, looking at me. "My brother has enough to help us start over again. We don't have to do this."

"Like hell we do," Billy said.

"No we don't," Tate said. "I don't want a life like this forever. We can change things…"

"Okay," Billy said. "Okay, so I wasted all my time getting to know this place, pretending to be the maintenance man in this building for a week so I can check out this apartment and the security system. I spent so much of my fucking time getting this ready, and now you're telling me it's a no go because what? You want a piece of your brother's girl's ass? You want to win her over like some kind of gentleman?" Billy leaned into me, grabbing my wrist and using his free hand to grope my breast. I struggled to get loose, but he was too strong.

"Let her go," Tate said.

"The only way to win over this girl, and I know, is aggressively. Trust me, she likes it rough. It turns her on…" He leaned in and licked my face with his long tongue. I tried to move my face, but he held it with a vice grip. Then he moved his mouth over to crush his mouth against me so hard that I thought I bit my lips until it bled.

Immediately, Tate was on Billy, wailing on him, while Billy punched Tate back.

I got a chance to step back while Tate and Billy went at each other. Billy was larger, stronger, and bigger. He tore off Tate's t-shirt, while Tate grabbed Billy's to pull him to him so he can punch him in the face. Billy blocked it, and punched Tate across the face. Tate stumbled back, and I can see him steady himself before standing tall, ready to fight Billy again.

He squared off his broad shoulders, his chest going up and down, causing his hard abs to ripple up and down. Like Collins, who had a tattoo of a dagger on his shoulder,

Tate had tattoos all over his body. I looked away. He really didn't have the body of a kid. As far as I knew, he was built like a fully grown man. He would have no problem finding himself a girlfriend once he's settled and no longer on the streets.

Billy rammed into him before Tate knew what hit him, and knocked Tate against the wall, where he slumped down into an unconscious heap.

My mouth was opened in shock. I knew I had to get out now. There was no way to reason with Billy, and the way he looked, like an angry bull, he wasn't done with his rampage yet.

I ran for the door, but he blocked it, catching me at my waist, and lifting me in the air. "Let go of me!" I cried.

"No, Sammy," he said. "I never had the satisfaction of sticking it in you, and it's haunted me all these years."

"Move on!" I shouted.

"Can't," he said. "You're my ideal girl, Sammy. No one else compares to you, and you've ruined that for me. I have to have you so I know."

"I'm not your ideal girl. I'm not anyone's ideal, Billy. Take me off that damn pedestal, and know I'm just a girl, a real life girl. Take me out of your sick fantasy world, please, Billy and let me go!"

He crashed into my bedroom, threw me onto the bed. He began unbuttoning his pants, unzipping it, then pulling it down.

I was suffocating. This was not sexy at all. This was not what I wanted.

"Now, I'll finally get to have you," Billy said, lunging towards me, and missing.

I grabbed the nearest heavy object... my Bose radio/alarm clock and chucked it towards him. It hit him on the head, and he was dazed for a while. I got up to run to the bedroom door, but he was quick enough to block it again. "I'm getting tired of you avoiding me," he said.

"It's not avoiding," I said. "It's running. I want nothing to do with you, Billy. Get that through your thick ape-like head!"

"I waited too long to let this go," Billy said. "Your Dad put me in jail, you know. Now I want revenge. I'll taint his precious pure daughter that he'd warned me away from. I'll make sure you're nice and dirty so no one will ever want you again!"

I tried not to listen to his threats. I knew he was trying to scare me, to get me to melt down and not fight back. But as soon as I stop fighting, I knew that would be it for me. This time, Billy wanted more than sex from me. He wanted me dead.

I bolted to the bathroom, closed the door, locked it, and then to the closet where the half-door to the Production Room was. I shifted through the gowns and found the door, opening it, making sure the gowns didn't look touched, and slipped through, locking the half-door behind me.

I turned around, facing the controls in the control room within the Production Room. How safe was I here? How long before Billy would find me in this hidden room?

I looked around…the room I was so afraid of had become my sanctuary.

I walked over to the Casanova bed…I was so tired. The exhaustion finally hitting me like a boulder as I laid on the comfortable luxurious bed. This was my chance to rest, to gather my strength again before I have to face Billy.

Finding You Finding Me (You & Me Trilogy #2)

I knew I was going to face him. I had to in order to move on.

Chapter 18

The half-door from the closet door shook violently against its hinges. Billy.

He had found the hidden door in the closet, and now he was trying to break the door down.

As the door rattle violently back and forth, I ran to the door on the other side, slid it open, and ran to the living room. Now was my chance to get out, while Billy was preoccupied. I got to the door, and before I could open it, the door flew open, revealing a worried Collins.

"Sam!" He called. "Thank God you're alright…" he stopped in mid-sentence as he looked around and assessed the room and situation. His eyes rested on the slumped body of Tate on the ground. Then, his eyes widened as he attempt to grab me to pull me outside of my apartment.

Finding You Finding Me (You & Me Trilogy #2)

I turned around, and it was Billy. And he was armed with a knife the size of a butcher's knife.

All my suspicions of Billy were confirmed. He was a raving lunatic. A madman. A psychotic criminal.

"Watch out!" Collins called, running towards me to push me out of the way of Billy's knife. The knife grazed Collins' shoulders, cutting through his suit, but missing any vital parts.

Collins turned around, stepped out of the way of Billy's arms, and grabbed Billy's wrist with lightning speed. He pulled Billy's arms into an angle against him that made it so painful, Billy's hands opened, causing the knife to drop to the ground.

Collins kicked the knife away, and Billy tried to retrieve his arm, but Collins held it tightly in his, still at an angle where he could easily break Billy's arm in half.

He used his leverage to bring Billy down to his knees. "Try anything right now, and you kiss your arm good-bye," Collins said, making Billy bow low.

Collins' eyes found mine, and it was full of love mixed with relief. "Come here, Sam," he said.

I walked over to where Billy was on his knees, bowing.

"Now, does this guy owe you an apology?" Collins asked.

I nodded.

"You heard what the lady said," Collins said to Billy. "Apologize."

"Oh, he'll need to do more than that," I said bitterly. I walked up to Billy and looked him in the eyes. "I could give into this overwhelming feeling of hate for you, Billy, for all the years of fear and loathing you've caused me, but I refuse to give you that power over me."

"Slut," Billy said when I had walked away.

"What?" I asked.

"Slut," Billy said. "For leading me on, for leading all men on, for being the dirty slut for that perverse SOB boyfriend you have there!" Billy winced. "Owe, man!"

Collins eyes seethed with anger, as he jerked Billy's arms up further, painfully.

"You keep going with that charming attitude, and I'll break your legs, too," Collins said. "Don't think I've never put a man into the emergency room clinging to his life before."

Collins nodded at the butcher knife on the ground where he kicked it. I went to pick it up to keep it out of reach from Billy and anyone else. "I carried a knife like that with me all the time, Kid," Collins said. "Was well-known on the streets as Daggers because of it. Anyone who messed with me, got a taste of my dagger. It's as simple as that."

"You're not so tough anymore, Suit!" Billy said.

"Want to test that theory out?" Collins said. "I can carve your initials on your penis so quickly, your penis would have whiplash."

"Yeah? You think you're so tough?" Billy asked. "Look how much fear I instill in her. She still trembles when she hears my name. That's real power."

Collins punched Billy's smug face once, stunning Billy, before he said, "You will live to regret ever doing that to Sam, asshole."

Collins looked at me again. His eyes tender with love. "What do you want to do to him, Sam? This is your closure. How would you like to grant retribution to this filth?"

I walk up to Billy. I wanted to stab him with the butcher's knife, right through the heart. I wanted to castrate him so he'd never try to rape another person again.

I reached over, ran my hand through his hair to the back of his head, grabbed his head and said, "For years you tormented me, made me cower just by hearing the sound of your name. For years you haunted me, never making me forget the memory of your filth. Today, you will let me go, as I will let all power you hold on me go." I leaned into him and spat into his face, "Where you're going, pretty boy, you'll make a real nice girlfriend for someone. Guess who's the bitch now?" I rammed his face down on my knees so hard, I swear the entire building could hear me break his jaw before he slumped to the ground.

*****

The police swarmed the room soon after, and Billy was handcuffed and taken away, while a nurse was called in to tend to Tate when Collins and I decided not to press charges on him.

"I saw everything," Tate whispered to me when I stopped by to check in on him. "Collins...wow. He's amazing. I've never seen moves like those before. And you, you're amazing. Who knew you were such a fighter...you're so petite."

"Strength comes in many sizes," I said. "I didn't know I was so strong until I was tested. I guess I'm just now finding out more about myself because of it."

"Do you mean what you said earlier about me moving in with you and Collins and helping me get a new start?" he asked, his eyes pleading. His mask was off now, and I was still getting used to the fact that I knew him from Sawyer House. Pierced boy. I didn't like what he did there, but then again, him being a prankster was consistent to what he knew, especially when he had a criminal like Billy for a role model. He was the boy I was supposed to train to become a peer counselor. He was "Billy" the kid who told me guys were calling Sawyer House to get their jollies off, talking to me.

"Nothing is guaranteed," I said. "You'll have to make most of the effort, Tate, if you want to turn your life around. You can't blame anyone else for the way your life turned out. Not anymore. If you're serious about wanting to start over again, you have to do everything you can, change your way of thinking, change habits, whatever it takes to turn that around, to get there. Collins and I will only be a support group along the way, but most of the work is on you, do you understand?"

Tate nodded.

"Then I'll talk to Collins about it," I said.

Chapter 19

After Tate left with a social worker, Collins turned to me. He looked tired and as exhausted as I felt. He fell on the sofa, and pulled me to him, wrapping his arms around me tightly, while kissing my forehead.

"Baby," he said. "Want to talk about it?"

"What?" I asked, snuggling up to him and resting my face against his chest.

"Was that jerk the reason why you had issues with intimacy, with me touching you the first time we were together?" he asked.

I never told Collins about the Billy Incident. I never really told anyone about it, hiding it within me, too afraid to acknowledge it was there. 'Yes," I said.

Kailin Gow

"I kinda figured that out," Collins nodded. "From the way you froze up around him. He put some major juju into you, didn't he?"

"Collins," I said, unable to suppress a smile at the word "juju", which I would bring up later some day with him, "Billy stalked and tormented me throughout school, threatening to hurt anyone I cared about or slashing my throat if I'd ever tell. He would grab me in the hallway, pulled me into the bathroom and force me against my will to do things to him, and he would fondle me on threat of hurting me, on the threat of hurting Nydia."

Collins eyes filled with tears as he realized what I was telling him. This was my Achilles heel, the guilt and shame I had carried with me throughout the years. The reason why I had so much fear in me. "I'm so so sorry," he said hugging me tighter. "No wonder why you're so afraid of me touching you. No wonder why you would break down at the thought of having sex." He kissed my lips softly, and then my forehead. "I'm so sorry I didn't understand. Now I know."

"I wanted to tell you, Collins, but I honestly forgot some of the details. The last time I saw Billy was when he tried to rape me at my father's old church. It was so traumatic, I couldn't handle it, that any memories of it got pushed back into my subconscious. It wasn't until I met you, and you evoked such feelings of passion in me that these feelings surfaced."

"I never thought I could feel anything again after that," I continued. "I didn't think I could get intimate with anyone and have a real romantic relationship," I said. "So for the longest time, I avoided it. I stayed friends with every guy I met, even if I thought I could take it further than friendship. I was too scared to venture beyond friendship and into anything that would be too intimate. Until I met you, Collins." I sighed, taking in Collins' warmth, his beauty, and his vulnerability. Seeing Tate today was like seeing a younger lost Collins. Now I understood what his life was like before he was found. It was a living hell, but from that, emerged the beautiful complex man that I was now in the arms of.

Collins answered by kissing me on the lips, a lingering kiss that showed how much he wanted me to know he loved and supported me. "You are an amazing woman, Sam. You could have become a bitter person, a shy recluse, or even a bully like Billy yourself; but you turned that incident into a triumph for everyone, including you. You became a better person, helping other people deal with their issues. I'm so very proud of you," he said.

"But what about Tate?" I asked. Now that I've met him, I felt I couldn't just let him fall into the cracks and become lost like the other young promising kids, who could have turned out like Collins.

"So you've met Tate," Collins said. "Charming, isn't he?"

"I didn't think so when he pulled a prank on me at Sawyer House, but I have to admit even while being in danger from him while he was here in our apartment, I couldn't help caring for him." I touched Collins' cheeks. "He has your charm, Collins. I think he can change, turn his life around like you did at his age."

"You know I was planning on having him live with me at the Newport Coast home I have there and having him enroll at your high school. But you will not be his tutor, as I originally planned, nor be bait for him." Collins sighed. "Although I think he's already hooked. From the way he was talking about you when I sent him off tonight with a social worker, I think he may be a little half in love with you."

"Psst! Nonsense," I said. "That's just because you're my boyfriend so you think everyone is after your girlfriend."

"Every guy I met around you seemed to be," Collins said.

"Maybe I have pheromones," I joked. "Like Cleopatra."

Collins leaned in, smelling me, "No, not pheromones. You don't smell like honey, but," he kissed me, his tongue touching the corners of my mouth before delving in. "You taste like honey, so sweet, and nourishing."

"Nourishing?" I asked. "Very sexy, you know."

"It is to me," Collins said. "You in a potato sack with green hair would be sexy to me."

I turned around and placed my arms around Collins' neck, and kissed him long and hard. Any man who thought

Kailin Gow

I looked sexy with a potato sack on while having green hair is a man who loved me on my best days and on my worse.

Despite how tired we both were, we continued kissing heavily into the night until we fell asleep in each other's arms, our lips touching.

Chapter 20

I didn't bring up what I heard in the Courthouse between Collins and Judge Colleen Seevers. I wanted to trust Collins that nothing happened, that Colleen Seevers came unto him, and that was it.

But another trip to the Courthouse, this time about Tate's custody and guardianship, made me think twice. Of all the cases like this, why did Colleen Seevers have to be the judge on these. It wasn't fair how much control she had over everyone, especially on Collins.

It wasn't fair she was taking advantage of Collins over these favors.

I didn't know what was going on, but when I accidentally picked up Collins' phone lying next to mine on the nightstand, while he was in the showers, I saw a text message from Colleen Seevers to Collins.

CS: That favor you asked of me, considered it done. Tate'll be released under your guardianship. Now for a favor in return, you know what I want. Meet me at Casanova Club. Usual spot.

I knew I shouldn't do it, but I had to know, so I texted back.

CollinsM: What do you have in mind?

She took the bait.

CS: Some heavy loving, lover boy.

My blood boiled beyond control. How dare she? Collins was with me! How dare she use her position of power to make Collins sleep with her? My poor Collins. I knew he would do it just because he was trying to help me with Nydia and now Tate. I couldn't let him do this.

Finding You Finding Me (You & Me Trilogy #2)

I had to help Collins break free from women who were using him purely for sex like Colleen Seevers was doing. She had a hold on him, that must have stem way back to when he was young and vulnerable. I had to confront this woman and get her claws off of him.

I texted back.

CollinsM: When? Date? Time?

CS: Tomorrow night. Find an excuse to meet me. I'm desperate for your tongue fucking.

My stomach curled and I suppressed my urge to text her back a go F Yourself message.

Instead, I text back.

CollinsM: All this pleasure for me? I should ask you for more favors, Judge.

CS: Lover Boy, you are the best. Can't wait.

I sent the text thread over to me. Then deleted her text messages.

I knew Collins would be upset if he found out what I planned to do, but it was for his own good. This woman would no longer have an emotional and physical hold on him, if I can help it.

It was time to set Collins free. This was the first step. He'd helped free me from my imprisonment, now it was my turn to return the favor.

Epilogue

I stepped into the lavished club done in Italian Renaissance décor. This was the Casanova Club. I didn't know what I was doing here, except I wanted to confront the woman who was Collins' own version of Billy. From the conversation I gleamed that day in the courthouse, this woman took away Collins' innocence; she abused him, took advantage of him when he was a minor and she was the judge of his case. It was time to put a stop to her hold on him.

I asked where the usual spot was for Colleen Seevers from one of the hostesses dressed in a Burlesque outfit, and she directed me to a table where the woman I came to confront sat in a tight black leather corset top and leather black pants. I gulped. She was a Dom. I was so out of my league. Did I actually think I can talk her out of seeing Collins?

Colleen Seevers took one look at me and smiled. "I was expecting you, Kitty," she said.

"What?" I croaked. What had I gotten myself into. How did she know I was coming?

"Collins never answers me by text," she said. "So I thought it was you. So you want to play, Kitty?" She got up and came over to me, towering over me in her six-inch heels. "Looks like you need to be taught a lesson. Collins hasn't trained you, yet," she said, "or you wouldn't have any problems with him. But you see, you being what you are, an innocent is causing him a lot of pain. He can't have you this way. Sooner or later, Kitty, he'll leave you or get tired of you...so the choices you have are: leave him now and go away or join us here and be trained to be exactly what he wants and needs...consider it a lesson in love." She ran her emerald green eyes down my face, neck, and cleavage, looking like she wanted to devour me. "Collins sure knows how to pick them. You are a treat. A virgin, gorgeous, and just what I had wanted to play with for years. No wonder Collins latched onto you like a possessive puppy. You are a catch. It would be my pleasure training you." She licked her lips before she brought down the rod in her hands hard against the table. "What will it be?"

I gulped, wishing the floor would swallow me whole. What have I gotten myself into now all for the sake of love?

You & Me Series continues with Sam, Daggers, Derek, and Collins in Book 3

Freeing You Freeing Me
Summer 2013

About Kailin Gow

Kailin Gow was a peer counselor at the Women's Center during her undergraduate years. She produced and hosted a women's issues radio show and ran workshops and seminars in the community for women covering women's issues including self-esteem, sexuality, identity, and gender roles. She was an intern at Juvenile Court, working for the public defenders with teen charges. As an undergraduate at UC Irvine, she was also teacher's assistant in Criminology and Constitutional Law.

Never thinking she would be interested in the topic, she took her human sexuality class in college, and aced it, being voted by her group as the girl most of the classmates wanted to be stranded with on an island. She'd like to think it was because she knew so much about the subject, of course, not just because the college class was made up of mostly men.

Kailin Gow today is the author of several books for women, New Adults, and Young Adults. She has sold over millions of books. She divides her time living in the OC, Las Vegas, Dallas, and London, England with her Alpha husband and her Bad Ass in Training little girl.

Other Adult Romance Series from Sparklesoup Authors

Master Chefs Series

HEAT Serial

Kings of Fire Series

Loving Summer Series

Hidden Falls High Series

Kailin Gow

Inner Circle Series

Never Knights Trilogy

Blue Room Serial

Blue Room Confidentials

Saints of San Angelo U.

The Protégé

Barely Legal Serial

Sessions Serial

Finding You Finding Me (You & Me Trilogy #2)

Filthy Dirty Laundry

You & Me Trilogy

Rock Hard Musical

Drama Diaries Standalone Novels

Beautiful Girl: A Beauty and Beast Re-telling

Shadowlight Academy

Shadowlight Hunters Academy

Vampire Samurai Series

Kailin Gow

Society of Supernatural Sleuths

M.A.G.E. Series

Magical World Series

Fallen Fae Academy

Fae B. I. Series

Cruel Princes of Wyvern Academy

Ruthless Reign Series

Bad Boys Billionaire Bachelors Club

Finding You Finding Me (You & Me Trilogy #2)

The More the Merrier RH Series

Baby Girl Series

Bad Boys Royals of Kingsbury Prep

Kingmakers of Kingsbury

Prickly Proposal

HOUSE Series

Heartbreak Falls Series

The Bully Who Loved Me

Kailin Gow

OTHER ROMANTIC COMEDIES BOOKS

BOSSY BODYGUARD by Sunny Winters

https://www.amazon.com/BOSSY-BODYGUARD-Sunny-Winters-ebook/dp/B07B26CLQG

COCKY COP by Sunny Winters

https://www.amazon.com/COCKY-COP-Romantic-Sunny-Winters-ebook/dp/B07B2C4BVN

AFTERNOON DELIGHT by D.R. LOVE

https://www.amazon.com/Afternoon-Delight-D-R-Love-ebook/dp/B07B26NQH1

Finding You Finding Me (You & Me Trilogy #2)

TONGUE TIED by D.R. LOVE

https://www.amazon.com/Tongue-Tied-D-R-Love-ebook/dp/B07B263X98

JUNK by D.R. LOVE

https://www.amazon.com/JUNK-D-R-Love-ebook/dp/B07B23F9XJ

EATING VELVET by D.R. LOVE

https://www.amazon.com/Eating-Velvet-D-R-Love-ebook/dp/B07B29WLW8

STEPBROTHER FIGHTER by Rachel Angel

https://www.amazon.com/Stepbrother-Fighter-Steps-Standalone-Novel-ebook/dp/B07B24W4VL

OH MY! RAPTURE by A.B. Binds

Kailin Gow

https://www.amazon.com/Oh-My-Rapture-B-Binds-ebook/dp/B07B22WBGZ

Sign Up for My Newsletter

No spam. No ham. We only send you up-to-date information about new releases, new series, series updates, contests, author events and more at:

Steamy Adult Books

Kailin Gow

EXCERPT

Falling for

Summer

kailin gow

A Loving Summer Novel

Prologue

Love hits you when you least expect it, grabs you, sucks you in whole, and twists you around until you could hardly breathe. Love hurts like a sucker punch, that's both glorious and beautiful. Falling for Summer was like that for me, every time. - Nat Donovan

Nat

Several Months After Summer

There are demons in my family.

I know that because of what came down during the summer we returned to the Pad in Malibu and stayed with Aunt Sookie and Summer several months ago.

.

Plenty happened, and that's another story. What I'm here to talk about is what happened afterwards and how we're all trying to pick up the pieces the best we can. By "we," I mean me, my younger siblings, Drew and Rachel, who are fraternal twins, and my parents, who I refer to as Mom and Dad. We're the Donovans, and although it seems we have the perfect family on the surface, it's far from perfect. I'm the first to attest to that...as I've learned last summer. Me, Nathaniel Donovan, the oldest of the three Donovan siblings, the older of the Donovan Brothers, had a meltdown. It was brief, but it happened, and if it wasn't for Summer being there, it would have been worse. She made things better by being there for me, like always, selfless and giving, very loving. Like her Aunt Sookie, she is the most giving person I know, emotionally and demonstrably.

And with Summer, also physically. There's where I feel bad about the whole thing, like I'm not supposed to feel so attracted to Summer, but I am. I've known her since we were toddlers, but now it's different, and as soon as I've tasted her mouth. It tasted like honey and cinnamon as soon as my tongue met hers, I couldn't get enough of her. I wanted her, wanted to tear off her clothes and run my tongue up and down her body and fill her with all of me. By sheer will power I was able to pull back. But now there is that awkwardness between us, and that tension, and mostly that *guilt*. She was the angel who could calm my demons, yet arouse them at the same time, and I don't think I will be able to hold back the next time we get that close.

So I've been avoiding her, except for an occasional email or text about how she's doing or about Aunt Sookie's Acting Academy, which she inherited. According to Sookie's will, we Donovans have the obligation as partners to help out. But avoidance only makes my heart search harder, and although I'm trying to avoid her in all controllable aspects of my life, I can't stop thinking and dreaming of her. As it is with the one I'm having right now.

The air around me is as hot and thick as a wool blanket pulled up over my face. Sweat glistens on my skin... I can feel the stickiness form a film where my skin is exposed to the cooling night air. It's too hot, and so I work to kick off the sheets entangling my body, placed there a few hours earlier, more suitable for a cold fall evening in San Francisco. I'm too tired to keep my eyes open, caused by a marathon of all-nighters, preparing for my first semester exams. Except for the way my body's reacting, I could sleep like a zombie, but I can't. My body's reacting too much to the dream. If I were awake, if I weren't so damn tired, I could open my eyes and take control over the situation, but I'm not. So I'm still in the middle of that dream again...the dream that ends in a nightmare.

It's the one where I'm with Summer in her room the night she has on that slinky barely-there peach dress going out to see that actor Astor Fairway at his house for dinner, and maybe something more. Yup, it's that night a few months ago last summer when my life once again converged with Summer's in such a way, it seems like the three years of not seeing her before, never happened. When you've known someone for so long, practically grow up with them, live with them, stay with them, every summer for a decade or most of your life as it is for us Donovans and Summer, missing three years, can be erased in a heartbeat.

And in its place is the same feeling you felt three years ago, at your last encounter. Seeing Summer this past summer, brought back all of my memories...the good and the bad, the ugly and the beautiful.

Finding You Finding Me (You & Me Trilogy #2)

Seeing her dressed like that for some guy she just met, albeit a famous guy, just brought out the crazy side of me. It's irrational, but I guess that's what it's like for me when I feel so much for her, yet I can't have her. She may have a childhood crush on me, but she's off-limits. Not like Drew is off-limits to her because Rachel wouldn't want Summer hurt by Drew, but because she's Aunt Sookie's niece, and because Aunt Sookie has instilled it into my head to watch out for little Summer and the twins. That hasn't stopped me from falling for her, though.

She was beautiful, possessing sparkling green eyes and soft-to-the touch silky chestnut hair, with gently sun-kissed caramel highlights. Growing up, I used to make excuses to touch her hair… hair so soft and silky, it lit up moonless nights and smelled like waterfalls and sweet flowers. Even as a seven-year-old, she had eyes that bewitched me, and made it hard for me to look away. At times, they were smiling. At other times, they were crying. But at all times, they bore deep into me, reaching depths as deep as the ocean where we shared countless sunsets.

Now my dream shifts to another time before that night she stayed over at Astor Fairway's canyon home. Summer appeared before us at the airport last summer, where Drew, Rachel, and I laid eyes on her for the first time in years. Wow – just wow, how much she had grown.

Every part of me became well-aware of how Summer had grown. In three short years, she had blossomed into a stunningly attractive young woman. Funny how three years could alter so much. Like Drew, Summer has matured physically, from being a fun and cute girl with sparkling eyes, braces, dimples, and wavy, sometimes frizzy hair, to a jaw-dropping Victoria's Secret beauty. Looking over at Drew, who seemed to have lost his voice for a second, it appeared I wasn't the only one who had these thoughts.

For the Lothario that he was, he seemed uncharacteristically at a loss for words as we made our way over to Summer, where she was talking to Rachel. For a moment, I think he even took a deep breath before he stopped in front of her, his face flushed more than usual. His blue eyes staring at her with such intensity, it didn't take a rocket scientist for anyone to see that Drew still had a thing for Summer.

I nearly laughed witnessing the irony. He had become the man at school whom all the girls sought to tame, wanted to score with, had even been coined having a Drew Effect on. He was that male model you saw in muscle magazines with a face and physique that would make leading men blush. Chiseled, sculpted, and muscular, without an ounce of fat on him and having that perfect "v", he could be the model for any Adonis statue. He's that guy who women of all ages would drop everything to have sex with and not care whether or not he'd call her afterwards. He's Drew, and he had that kind of effect on women…every one of them except Rachel and one girl -- Summer.

There was something about Summer that always seem to make everything better. She has that healing touch, that gentleness and loving nature that was so like Aunt Sookie's. I had tried to avoid her and treat her like a kid sister but she had to grow up before my eyes and become a stunner like that. I avoided her alright, like a cold heartless fish…until the night she came out of her room, dressed as sexy as hell, and was headed out to have dinner at Astor Fairway's house. Dressed the way she was, I knew it wouldn't be just dinner Astor would have on his mind. Dressed like that, I wouldn't be surprised if Astor would skip dinner and go straight to dessert…Summer being the decadent dessert any guy would crave.

To hell with all the reasons why I couldn't be with Summer. All those years of resolve shot down with one glance at the curve of her breasts, her long tanned legs, her glistening lips. Damn, I couldn't help myself, seeing her in that slinky silk dress that showed off her soft, golden tan skin…skin I have long to touch and kiss since that moment I saw her again at the airport. She was, for lack of a better word, stunning. So much so, all my resolve to keep my distance from her, dissolved. The well broke, and like a starving man who had kept his feelings and desire in for a long time (three years at least!), I had confronted her.

If she were a chocolate bar, I would have torn off the wrapper and eaten her whole, then go back and lick every last delicious bit of chocolate left clinging to the wrapper over and over again.

Finding You Finding Me (You & Me Trilogy #2)

The dress showed off her curves and skin in a way I had to clench my hands to keep from wanting to reach out and touch her, to pull her to my chest and run my fingers through the caramel waves framing her face, and smash her luscious full mouth against mine.

With Summer, I'm wracked with feelings of intense desire and want. I've dated a few girls and even went far with them, but I've never wanted anyone in bed more than I wanted Summer, and I know it's wrong. We grew up together. She's my little sister's best friend, and she's Sookie's niece. We're like family. And she's always looked up to me like an older brother. I know Drew really liked her in that way, too, but he's Drew, and to him, he doesn't have an issue with crossing boundaries. All girls to him, except Rachel, are fair game. But I'm not like Drew, and falling for Summer is something I have to avoid. It'll be easy if I can shut my feelings off, easy if I just don't care, but when Summer looks at me with those eyes, and she moves close to me and puts her hands on my shoulder or touches my face, it takes more resolve than I can muster up. She's the part of me that I'm missing, the part of me that completes me. She makes me feel tenderness, gentleness, peace, and even a little bit of hope. She's like a dove, but not quite a helpless defenseless dove, but a steady and strong lioness who has the gentleness of a dove. That's a rare quality to find in a woman. I guess that's another reason I fell for Summer.

****

That night I tried to stop Summer from going out with Astor dressed like that, didn't end well, for me. She shot me down and went off on her date with Astor anyways, even staying over. Was it to spite me?

My mind tortured me with scenes of her with Astor, scenes of her kissing Astor, of Astor taking off that dress and doing everything to her that I wanted to do to her. I fell asleep dreaming of that as I was dreaming of it now. Only this time, instead of me feeling tortured, there was someone else. I saw another figure in that dream, watching Summer with Astor. Hidden by shadows. I couldn't see his face, but I felt his pain. Somehow we were connected in some way, and it was a pain harder than mine...a pain deeper than mine. Was it me in the shadows?

Finding You Finding Me (You & Me Trilogy #2)

When I turned around, the figure stepped out. It wasn't I, but someone else.

It was Drew, and he had a gun cocked to his head with a look so full of pain and anguish, tears flowing down his face, right before he fired.

Falling for Summer (Loving Summer #2/Donovan Brothers #1) – New Adult Version Now Available through Amazon Kindle. Adult Version Coming Soon!